40 DAYS TO ETERNITY

40 DAYS TO ETERNITY

JOE GARNER TURMAN

TATE PUBLISHING & Enterprises

Published by Tate Publishing & Enterprises, LLC
127 E. Trade Center Terrace | Mustang, Oklahoma 73064 USA
1.888.361.9473 | www.tatepublishing.com

Tate Publishing is committed to excellence in the publishing industry. The company reflects the philosophy established by the founders, based on Psalm 68:11,
"The Lord gave the word and great was the company of those who published it."

Book design copyright © 2011 by Tate Publishing, LLC. All rights reserved.
Cover design by Leah LeFlore
Interior design by Lindsay B. Behrens

Published in the United States of America

ISBN: 978-1-61777-180-4
1. Fiction / Romance / Historical   2. Fiction / War & Military
11.02.11

I

July 3, 1974, Hopewell, Texas

"John, I can't believe you won't be off for the Fourth." Betty pouched her lips in a pout. "Your boss and company are asking too much of you."

"Mom, we gotta keep those trucks rolling. As the main dispatcher, I've got to be there to keep things moving. It had to be either me or Harry Grimes, and he has a family, so I volunteered to be there. I'll try to knock off around ten thirty or eleven o'clock to eat lunch with the family."

Betty washed her hands in the kitchen sink and dried them on a dishtowel.

She turned toward John and spoke with a softer voice.

"John, you know how we want you to be with us for special occasions. We missed you so much when you were away in Vietnam."

John licked his dry lips. *Now was the time to tell his mom about his plans to go to Vietnam to get Mai and bring her here. He'd have to do it sometime. He might as well do it now.* John's heart pounded. But even though he knew what would probably happen, he decided to act. John pushed his chair back and stood up from the kitchen table.

"Mom, I need to talk to you about something. I've been waiting to get you and Dad together, but I want to tell you now, and I'll talk to Dad later." John's throat tightened, but he plunged ahead. "I know what I'm about to say will, well, it may shock you. Please try to understand what I want to do."

Betty moved closer to her son.

"Mom, I want to go back to Vietnam and find the girl I fell in love with and bring her back here to be my wife. I really love her. I've thought about her every day since coming home. I won't be satisfied until I go back and get her."

Betty stepped backward. "But son, you have a job, a good job. How can you just take off and go back to Vietnam willy-nilly?"

"I've already talked to my boss, and he's willing to give me forty days off. I figured I might need more than a month."

The color drained from Betty Gunter's face. She stared at her son with a look of disbelief. John stood and pulled a chair away from the table. "Please sit down, Mom. Do you feel okay? I didn't want to shock you, but I want you to know my plans. I'm sorry I haven't told you before now."

John knew Betty had picked Linda Graham as the girl for him. She had projected him getting his college degree while Linda supported them with her teacher's salary. He was sure it had never occurred to her that he might get involved with a Vietnamese girl.

Voice wavering, Betty reached for the chair and slowly lowered herself. "I don't know what to say. I mean, I never imagined you having a Vietnamese girlfriend. I'm disappointed, John. You know, those people are so different from us. They look different, talk differently; they're not like us at all. It's hard for me to see a Vietnamese girl fitting in here with our family and friends."

"Mom, Mai speaks English, and she's intelligent. Mai means flower in her language. She's the most beautiful girl I've ever known, and she's a Christian. Mom, you'll really like her when you get to know her. She's modest and kind and polite."

"Well, I've heard Vietnamese girls are beautiful, but I'm sure they think and act differently. John, are you really serious about marrying her?"

" Mom, I love her."

"You mean you want to go all the way back to Vietnam to find her, marry her, and bring her back here?"

"Yeah, I do. I plan to go the end of February. I've already checked on flights to Saigon. I'm excited about the trip."

"John, you know there's still a war going on over there, don't you?"

"I know, but there's very little fighting around Saigon and Nha Trang. Those were secure areas while I was there."

Betty covered her face with her hands. "I knew you weren't happy here. I didn't know what was bothering you, but I knew there was something." Then she reached her hands toward him as if pleading for him to come to his senses. "It doesn't make sense to me for you to go all the way to Vietnam to bring back a girl when there are dozens of nice girls here."

"Mom, I don't want to hurt you and Dad, but this is something I've gotta do. I love Mai, and if she'll marry me, I'm going to bring her back."

"You know we love you, John, and we only want what's best for you. I do hope you'll change your mind. We'll talk with your dad about this later."

John went to his room and sat at his desk. He felt a sense of relief that he had told his mom about Mai. His telling her had clarified his plans in his own mind and had made him even more determined to carry them out.

His thoughts turned toward Vietnam and Mai. What was she doing? Did she have a boyfriend? Was she still working as a cashier and hostess at the hotel in Nha Trang? Now, he was even more anxious to return to Vietnam.

The face of the beautiful girl he'd fallen in love with in Nha Trang, shimmered in his mind. He could see the dimpled smile and the long, silky, black hair that framed her lovely oval face. The memory tugged at his heart.

He spent his year in Vietnam at the army base in Nha Trang. It was one of the most memorable years of his life, and the highlight was getting to know Mai.

John thought about the first time he met Mai. He went to downtown Nha Trang with his buddy, Chuck, to have dinner at the Vien Dong hotel and to dance to the music of a well-known band from Saigon. After dinner, Chuck danced with one of the hostesses while John remained at the table drinking coffee. A fresh-faced young woman came over to his table.

"You want more coffee, soldier?" she asked. Her beauty and gentle spirit so completely captivated him that he did not immediately reply.

She repeated, "You want more coffee, soldier?"

"Uh, yes, I want more coffee," John stammered. As she refilled his cup, she asked, "You no dance, soldier?"

"No. I don't like to dance. I'm no good at dancing."

"Me, too, no good at dancing."

"Maybe I can just talk with you," John said. "Can you sit down and talk?"

"Okay, I talk with you." She smiled. "But not now. Maybe later when other girl come to cashier."

"I'll wait for you."

Several months later, Mai's English had improved. John knew his time talking with her each week had contributed to that improvement.

John wanted to know all about Mai. One day he asked her, "Since you grew up near Dalat, why and how did you come to Nha Trang?"

"I grew up in the mountains near a small town called Lien. My father is a farmer who grows vegetables and fruit that we sell at the Dalat Market. Since I am the oldest child in the family, I helped on the farm. We had some hired hands, but I needed to help also."

"Why did you leave the farm?"

"After I graduated from high school, I decided to leave Lien and find work in another place. Since my aunt lives in Nha Trang, I decided to come here. My papa did not want me to come, but my mama persuaded him to let me come to Nha Trang to find work."

"How did you get the job here at the Vien Dong hotel?"

"When I first came to Nha Trang, I looked and looked for a job, but I could not find one. Then one day I met Lan, and we quickly became friends. Lan worked as a cashier, and she said the hotel wanted to hire an assistant cashier. I came with Lan, and they hired me."

John couldn't remember exactly when he fell in love with Mai. Maybe it was love at first sight.

2

August 9, 1974, Hopewell, Texas

John Gunter stood transfixed before the TV morning show, shock playing across his ruddy features. "He resigned! I can't believe it."

Most Americans had seen it dozens of times, but John, for the first time, saw President Nixon make his famous signature gesture, both arms raised above his head with fingers in a victory sign at the door of the helicopter. The commentator noted that Nixon left the White House for the last time. John joined his mom and dad at the breakfast table.

"I didn't know the Watergate deal was so serious. I'm sure behind on the news."

Vance Gunter looked up from his morning paper. "Yeah, you sure are. The past two weeks since you've been working day and night, a lot of things have happened. Hey, I just made a pot of coffee. Grab a cup."

Sun-tanned and trim, Vance Gunter looked more like John's older brother than his dad. After graduation from high school, he served a tour in the army in 1946–49. Even though his job as

Hopewell's postmaster kept him busy, he found time to play tennis with John and his daughter, Debra. David, the youngest son, cared nothing about sports.

"John, you know when I was in the army in Germany, Richard Nixon was an ambitious young senator. Time does go by. As you know, I met your mom at North Texas State, and after we were married, we had to rake and scrape to get by. It was during the Truman presidency."

John said, "I guess I was born during that time."

"Yeah, you were and now you've served under Nixon in Vietnam."

Betty placed a plate of toast on the table. "Young man, you need to get on a more reasonable schedule. The world is passing you by."

I guess so, Mom. This coming Monday I'm back on my regular five-day-a-week schedule. I'm ready for it."

John glanced out the window at a biker on the street. In their middle-class neighborhood, the Gunter's ranch-style, four-bed-room, three-bath house blended well with the others on their block.

The Gunter family had moved to Hopewell in time for John to enroll for his first-grade class. Vance oversaw the building of their present house. John felt like he had lived in it forever.

Although John worked long hours, he enjoyed spending free time with Debra and David. They shot baskets, threw around the football and went to the popular young people hang-outs. David was a freshman at Texas Tech, and Debra graduated from North Texas State. She was preparing to teach first grade in a county elementary school nearby.

"I saw Linda Graham at school yesterday." Betty refilled John's cup. "We're getting ready for the new school year. She'll be teaching first grade. She asked about you. She's a nice, pretty girl."

John said, "I know Linda's happy to work with you as principal. You're the best principal around, I think."

"I don't know about that, but I did teach fifteen years at Hopewell Elementary before I became principal. I do know how things work."

"Linda should make a good teacher. She always made the best grades in our class. You know she was the valedictorian? We had forty who graduated … I wonder what's happened to everyone. You know Brad Parks from our class was killed in Vietnam. For a city of fifteen thousand people, Hopewell sure had its share of people to go to 'nam. It's sad that two never came back."

"You know I don't want to meddle in your affairs, John, but you should relax more. I know how you feel about that girl in Vietnam, but you ought to date more. Since you came back from Vietnam, more than a year ago, you've only gone out a few times. I think you should ask Linda for a date. She really likes you."

"Mom, you know how I feel about Mai. I do plan on marrying her and bringing her back here. " I did date Linda a few times in high school, but we were just friends. Our class did a lot of things together. We used to go to Clyde's for bowling and eating their greasy burgers and hotdogs. It was fun. Toward the end of the school year, we'd go to Dangler's Lake for swimming and water skiing."

John added, "Maybe some of us singles will get together after church Sunday and go bowling or get a burger or something."

Tuan Farm, Lien, South Vietnam

Mai Nguyen heard the news flash on the local radio station. She moved closer to the radio to hear over the chatter of her four siblings who jostled through the family room on their way to school. The news was of no concern to most residents of Lien or the other small towns and villages in the Central Highlands of South Vietnam. The American president, Richard Nixon, resigned from his office.

But the news caught Mai's attention and stirred her memory of John Gunter, the American soldier she loved—and still loved. It seemed like only yesterday they walked on the beach in Nha Trang.

"Mai, what'ta ya gonna do with the seashells in that sack?" he asked her. "I'm taking them to my brothers and sisters."

"Don't they have seashells there?"

Mai laughed. "Of course not. We live in the mountains."

John fell to his knees in an effort to catch a sand crab. The crusty creature darted, changing direction with amazing quickness that left John holding a handful of sand.

Mai smiled at John's efforts. "Be glad you did not catch it. Crabs pinch."

Walking further down the beach, Mai's mood changed though she hoped John would not sense it.

"Is something wrong?" he asked. "You suddenly seem so sad."

"I just remembered that you will soon go back to America."

"Yeah, I'll be leaving at the end of next month. We'll be one of the last American Army units to leave Vietnam."

Mai walked several steps in silence. "Will you come back?"

"Sure I'm coming back. It'll take a while, though. I'll get my discharge from the army the last week of June. Then I'll find a job to make enough money to come see you. When I come, I want to meet your family."

"I will be very sad when you go, John, but I will be very happy when you come back."

After he returned to the States, John wrote Mai several times, but her replies suddenly stopped. John didn't know Mai had left Nha Trang to return to her father's farm in Lien. And Mai was not aware that John's letters were returned to him because no one knew where to forward them. Mai assumed John forgot her. But Mai still loved John and treasured the memories of the time spent with him. She wondered where he was and what he was doing. Did he have another girlfriend? Would he really come back? If he did, would he search for her?

American Club, Nha Trang, South Vietnam

Ted Danner had a serious look on his usually smiling face. Ted and a missionary friend, Jeff Burt, met every Thursday for lunch at the American Club in Nha Trang.

The American Club catered to the foreign community, especially Americans. The noon menu featured hamburgers, pizza, and spaghetti. The club provided a cool retreat from the sweltering coastal heat. Its thick red carpets and black mahogany tables gave it a country club atmosphere. As Ted and Jeff moved toward their favorite table, they heard muffled undertones of dozens of conversation, but today no laughter.

Ted and Jeff usually discussed politics and the military situation in Vietnam. With a master's degree in history from the University of Minnesota, Ted enjoyed sharing his insights. His quiet voice belied how strongly he felt about recent developments.

"Jeff, pack your bags. We're not going to be here much longer."

"What are you saying?"

"You heard the news this morning, didn't you? Richard Nixon has resigned. You know what that means, don't you?

"What do you think it means, that Hanoi is now coming after us?"

Ted nodded. "You nailed it. The North Vietnamese will be coming. It's only a matter of time. Keep your suitcases packed. Their fear of Nixon is the only reason they haven't come sooner. They knew if they crossed the Seventeenth Parallel Nixon would bomb them back to the Stone Age."

"The South has all kinds of war materials left by the American Army. Shouldn't they be able to make a fight of it," Jeff asked.

"Do you really think they can or will?"

"I don't know. Based on what I've seen and heard, I have my doubts."

Ted nodded in agreement, "The North Vietnamese Army is motivated and will fight on a handful of rice. They'll be coming, and I don't know if the South will be able to stop them."

"Yeah, I'm afraid you're right. I'll bet Nixon's resignation has already caused a stir in Hanoi.

Ted said, "Hey, I just got a letter from John Gunter. You probably remember him? He's a tall, easy-going guy who was stationed here in the army."

Jeff screwed up his forehead, "Naw, I don't remember him."

"Well, John is coming back to Vietnam to try to find the girl he was dating while he was here. She worked at the Vien Dong Hotel as a cashier and went to the Protestant Church. I met John at the Sunday night English service. He came to me one time for counsel about marrying this girl. He's planning on coming back next January or February."

Jeff said, "His timing is not good. It's getting more insecure every day. With Nixon's resignation, I expect things to get worse."

"Yeah, I agee with you."

3

Politburo, Hanoi, North Vietnam

After President Nixon resigned, other events begin to unfold on the world's stage that would place John Gunter and Mai Nguyen in the middle of these tumultuous happenings. A meeting took place in Hanoi that would affect nations and millions of people. Two people in love, John and Mai, were not aware of this meeting, but their lives would be impacted by that rather brief morning conference at the Politburo in Hanoi, North Vietnam.

Communist Party First Secretary Le Duan nodded upon greeting his Politburo peer, General Vo Nguyen Giap. Le Duan stood erect in his neat, gray, high-collared uniform. He looked younger than his sixty-seven years with only slight graying at the temples, and his smile displayed even white teeth.

"Please, sit down, comrade. I am glad you dropped by. I want to talk with you about recent developments."

"Thank you, comrade," answered General Giap. "I also want to talk with you. Your positive and aggressive spirit always inspires me."

"Thank you, Comrade Giap, but everyone knows it is your indomitable spirit that has ignited the will and determination of our army and people."

Le Duan looked to his aide standing nearby and nodded. The servant quickly left to prepare a tray of tea and cakes for the host and the visitor.

"Well, Comrade Giap, you look as strong and healthy as you did twenty-five years ago. You remember how zealous we were during those days of our war against the French invaders. Now I believe we are again going to be victorious just as we were in defeating the French at Dien Bien Phu."

"Yes, comrade, I agree with you. I believe the recent resignation of the American President, Richard Nixon, means the Americans are tired of Vietnam and will only give minimal support, if any, to the South. This is why I think we should be preparing our forces for an all-out invasion to end this war and unite our people."

"I think your assessment of the situation is correct, Comrade Giap; however, we must move wisely, for half of our comrades in the Politburo do not agree with us. They think our army is not large enough for an all-out invasion and that we do not have enough war materials for a sustained push into the South."

"They are quick to point out that the Russians are barely supporting us, so we are limited in our artillery and ammunition," General Giap replied.

Diminutive General Giap, the hero of Dien Bien Phu, sat quietly for a moment. He stood just over five-feet tall, and it was no secret that Napoleon was his hero. He wore the gray uniform with four stars on the high collar that designated him as commander in chief of the People's Army of the Republic of Vietnam.

"Yes, Comrade Duan, I know how they have studied and analyzed the situation. They want us to move cautiously and slowly so as to ensure victory. But you know, Comrade, and I know, victory comes by bold and aggressive action. Our victory will not depend upon the superiority of our weapons but upon the will and tenacity of our soldiers."

The aide returned with a laden tray. Le Duan gestured with an open hand over the table. "Please, Comrade, have some of our best tea from the mountains north of us and the best tea cakes in Hanoi."

The two graying leaders cuddled their hot teacups, sipping and savoring the fresh taste from the slopes near the China border. Le Duan placed his cup on the table and selected a square cake. He carried himself with an air of confident authority forged by his formative years spent in colonial jails. They made him a determined revolutionary.

Le Duan spoke slowly between bites. "Comrade, we have known one another for a long time. We are of the same mind and spirit. This is why I wanted to talk to you about the recent development in Washington. Like you, I believe this happening signals that we can get our forces ready for an all-out invasion of the South." He paused to emphasize his next point. "We will have opposition, but we can begin to move toward our goal. Let us be patient and wise, and we shall be rewarded."

When Mai first saw John in the hotel dining room, he attracted her. His easygoing manner was different from other American soldiers. Some were straightforward in their approach and wasted no time trying to date her. Others wanted to talk with her over a drink.

Her job as cashier gave her an easy way out of any dating relationships. When asked for a date or to dance, she said, "Thank you, but I am busy with my work."

Lan advised her about responding to customers, especially American soldiers. "Be nice and polite, but keep a business relationship. Remember, you are the cashier. Sometimes you will seat customers, but your main job is behind the counter."

The day John left to return to the US, Mai tried to carry on as usual, but her heart wasn't in it. Before long, she asked the hotel manager to excuse her from her job. "I want to return to my father's farm," she told him. "I'm homesick for my family."

Mai spoke the truth but not the whole truth. She was homesick, but she was also lovesick. She told Lan, "I think about John all the time. I see the table where he usually sat, and I think about him. I keep looking at the door thinking he's coming in, but I know he's not."

Would she ever see him again? She didn't know the answer, but she wanted to go back home and regroup.

Her manager liked her attitude, honesty, and diligence. He tried to persuade her to continue on as cashier, but her mind was set on returning to her father's farm.

Being back on the farm was an adjustment. Yes, the first week had been delightful in renewing relationships with family, but farm life was in stark contrast to the busy life in Nha Trang. Mai enjoyed relating to her peers, but in the Lien area, most girls her age were married with two or three children.

Her social life consisted of church activities. Many of the men in her age group were in the military or already married. There were a few unmarried men in the church, but they were ten or fifteen years older than Mai.

Minh cast his eyes at Mai. He let it be known to Mr. and Mrs. Tuan that he would like to marry her. Me Hanh suggested to Mai that Minh would be a good match for her because his family owned land and obtained a degree of prosperity through their vegetable gardens and Minh's other jobs. Mai said, "Mother, times are different now. Girls don't marry just for money and position. They want to feel attracted to the man, love him, and know he loves her."

"But that's not Vietnamese culture," Me Hanh answered. "Families don't arrange marriages as they did years ago, but families still play a role in the selection of mates and influence how serious they become."

"But Mother, young people have more freedom nowadays, especially in cities."

"I know, and this freedom idea comes from America and Europe. But our families are stronger here in Asia than in the West. Here every member of the family is accountable to the others."

"Mother, as a Christian, I am accountable to the Lord for how I live my life. I do want to honor you and Papa as my parents. I want your advice and wisdom in my life, especially in choosing a mate. But I only want to marry someone I truly love."

"Well spoken, daughter, and I believe God will lead you to the right person. However, you are also accountable to your family and friends. The person you marry affects others."

"Pastor Chanh says a Christian should only marry another Christian."

"Yes, I agree with our pastor," Me Hanh said, "because the Bible teaches that truth. God knows that if you marry someone who's not a believer, you will have continual conflict in your marriage."

"Mother, would you rather I marry a Vietnamese man who's not a believer or a foreigner who is a Christian?"

"Why are you asking me this difficult question? You know I would rather you marry a Vietnamese Christian. Marrying a foreigner makes marriage difficult."

"But Mother, if this foreigner was a Christian and we loved one another, I think it could be a good marriage. Do you not think so, Mother?"

"Yes, it might possibly work out. Are you thinking of marrying a foreigner? You know they don't fit in with our ways of doing things. And if the man took you to another country, you wouldn't look like them or talk like them."

"I would only marry a foreigner if he is a Christian and I love him and he loves me."

Me Hanh folded the children's school clothes and placed them in a neat pile on a table in the all-purpose room just off from the kitchen. "Ibu Hue asked me if you have a boyfriend. That's the second time she's asked about you. I told her you're in no hurry to get married. She's a bit nosy."

"That doesn't bother me, Mother. It seems to bother some older women if a young woman doesn't get married soon in life. I hope it doesn't bother you."

"No, I want you to wait for the right person."

"Mother, Minh keeps on coming here on some pretext of wanting something. But I have no interest in him. He's a hard worker, has been good to his mother, and has saved his money, but Minh is not the Minh I knew in school. There's a hardness about him. I liked him as a friend in school, but I never had any desire to date him."

"He's a good worker and looks after his mother. When he comes home from driving a truck for Hao he goes out to help his mother oversee the workers in their gardens. You know, it hasn't been easy for Minh. He was ten when his father was killed in Saigon. His older brother and sister went to school in Saigon, got jobs there, and only come back to visit once or twice a year. While they're here, they treat him like he's still a child."

"Mother, I hear rumors that Minh joined the National Liberation Front Party. Is that true?"

"I don't know about that. I do know that his mother is worried about him and some of the people that he's hanging around with at night."

"A classmate told me that Minh hates Americans. He thinks Americans were responsible for the death of his father."

"Mai, that's not true. His father was killed by President Diem's men while he was marching with a group of radical Buddhists. The Americans had nothing to do with it."

As the months passed and there were no letters from John, Mai made an adjustment in her thinking about the possibility that John would come back for her. She loved John and thought about him every day, but she begin to think about her life without him.

After almost two years, no one came into Mai's life that interested her. She plunged into working on the farm and helping her siblings. She spent more time in church activities and Bible studies than she did in the past. But somehow Mai never gave up hope that John would return. Somewhere deep inside her there arose a spark, a slight whisper, a feeling, yes, something more than a feeling, that she would see John again.

4

February 28, 1975, South Vietnam

John Gunter felt the creeping chill of uncertainty crawling up his spine as the plane leveled off for landing at Tan Son Nhut Air Base in Saigon. Was he wasting his time in coming back to Vietnam? Was he a fool to come not knowing whether Mai would be waiting?

Vance and Betty Gunter took him to Dallas to catch a flight to Los Angeles.

John never did like good-byes at airports. He felt uncomfortable with his mom and dad under the circumstances. Though his dad seemed to accept his return to Vietnam more than his mom, he knew neither of them approved.

When Vance Gunter served in Germany, he dated a German girl from an upper-middle-class family. Although their time together did not develop into a serious relationship, Vance could better understand his son falling in love with a foreigner. John and his father were alike not only in physical features, but also in temperament. Like his father, John was steady and easygoing. But when pushed, he could explode with a quick temper.

The call came to board the L.A. flight. John hugged his parents and joined the boarding line. When he glanced back, he was saddened to see tears on his mom's cheeks.

From L.A. he laid over several hours in Honolulu, flew to Hong Kong, and then on to Saigon. The airport and terminal looked the same as when he left Vietnam in March of 1973 with the last contingent of American troops. He saw the early morning crew sweeping out the terminal at a slow pace. Although it was only eight o'clock in the morning, the Saigon heat felt like a blast from an oven.

All of the odors of Vietnam that he remembered suddenly assaulted his nose. The sharp, brine smell of *nuoc mam,* the fish sauce the Vietnamese ate every day, coupled with the dank smell of the street forged a bridge back into his memories. Instead of being irritated, he embraced them as a welcoming committee to remind him he was back to carry out a mission.

After getting his luggage, he hurried to the counter and bought a ticket to Nha Trang on the 11:30 a.m. flight. Since he had plenty of time before his departure, he found an airport cafe and ordered a cup of coffee. The pretty waitress in the traditional Vietnamese *ao dai* served him. She reminded him of Mai.

After boarding his flight, John felt a rush of excitement. He would soon see Mai. He looked out the window as the Air Vietnam plane began to circle the Nha Trang Airport. When the plane leveled off for the final descent, he could see the palm trees and the wide, white sandy beach. He spotted his former Army base that was now garrisoned by the South Vietnamese Army.

He tried to get a glimpse of the Vien Dong Hotel in the downtown area, but he could not see it out his window. He would be there in a few minutes.

Politburo, Hanoi

Even as John Gunter flew into Nha Trang and Mai Nguyen worked on her father's farm, events were taking place that would put them in the severest crucible of their young lives. Decisions were confirmed in Hanoi that would impact South Vietnam in ways the world would never imagine.

The Communist Party First Secretary, Le Duan, leaned forward in his chair to emphasize his point to General Vo Nguyen Giap.

"Yes, we were right, comrade. We were right. In the December Politburo meeting, we pushed for a more aggressive campaign in the South. Our southern commanders also wanted a bolder strategy."

General Giap responded with a smile. "The southern commanders were justified in that they have taken Phuoc Binh City and, indeed, the entire Phuoc Long Province."

"Many of our peers in the Politburo worried about the response of the Americans. You remember we told them then that the Americans would do nothing because they are paralyzed politically and militarily."

"The Americans are out of this war," General Giap agreed. "We can unleash our troops. General Dung should be arriving in the South today to lead an all-out offensive against Thieu's troops. I have full confidence in him. As you know, General Van Tien Dung was my chief of staff at Dien Bien Phu."

Le Duan nodded in affirmation. "I also have full confidence in General Dung. After all, you, General Giap, were his mentor. He will, like you, carry out a bold strategy. Yes, comrade, we will soon hear great things about General Dung and his forces."

February 28, 1975, Nha Trang

John took a taxi to go to the Vien Dong Hotel in downtown Nha Trang where Mai worked. On the way, he passed his former base. He saw the guards at the gate. On his right was the beach

He remembered the many times he and his buddies relaxed on the beach playing touch football, swimming, pitching horseshoes, and picnicking. It provided a good place to get away from the daily military routine.

When he arrived at the hotel, his heart was pounding. He was about to see Mai. How would she receive him? Sweat dripped off his forehead and his chest felt tight. He went into the restaurant, but the young woman behind the counter was not Mai. He greeted her and then asked, "Where is Mai?"

The young woman did not speak English. Answering him in Vietnamese, she realized he did not understand, so she went looking for someone who could speak English. She came back with a woman dressed in traditional long dress. John did not recognize her. She spoke very little English.

"You look for Mai?"

"Yeah, I want to see Mai. Where is she?"

"Mai not here now. She go back to Dalat."

"Where does she live in Dalat?"

"We not know where. She been gone long time."

"Is there anyone here who would know where Mai lives? I know she came from a small village near Dalat."

"I not know. We not know. Mai not come back here."

A wave of disappointment swept over John. Suddenly all the tension and fatigue from the long trip flowed through his body. He sat down at the nearest table, and a waitress came to take his order. His last meal had been on the flight. He felt empty.

Looking over the menu, he was reminded of the French influence on Vietnamese foods. He ordered a chateaubriand steak with the trimmings. After eating, he felt better so he checked into the hotel and walked up to his room on the second floor. He sank down onto the soft mattress and fell asleep.

John woke in the dark room. He lay still for a few moments trying to remember where he was. When he heard the plaintive voice of the pho peddler hawking his noodle soup on the street below, he realized he was in Nha Trang.

He glanced at his watch. It was four o'clock. He could hear people stirring about on the street. The pho peddler's call drifting through his window reminded him that he wanted food but not noodles. John took a shower and went down to the restaurant to get breakfast. He ordered two eggs, a pork chop, and coffee. He recalled that you could not find American-style bacon in most Vietnamese restaurants, nor toast. But the French bread was better.

Over his second cup of coffee, John thought about his plans for the day. He needed to find someone who knew the location of Mai's village. If he just went to the Dalat area without knowing where to go, he would waste a lot of time and energy. Who would know the location of Mai's home village?

He remembered Mai's friend Lan. Did Lan still work at the hotel? He looked around for the woman from the previous night who spoke some English. He saw her serving at another table. When she turned and headed back toward the kitchen, John asked her, "Does Lan still work here?"

"Lan? No, she no work here now."

"Where does she live?"

"She live in Phouc Hai."

John paused, trying to remember the location of Phouc Hai.

"Where is Phouc Hai?"

"Phouc Hai near airport. You take taxi or cycle. They take you to Phouc Hai."

"What street does she live on in Phouc Hai? What is her address?"

"Me not know. Lan live in Phouc Hai. You go ask. Okay?"

John looked for a taxi. Several drivers waited in front of the hotel. One knew that an American was looking for a taxi to take him to Phouc Hai. He approached John. "I take you to Phouc Hai for cheap price. You go now?"

After agreeing on a price, John got in the front seat so he could talk to the driver. Most taxi drivers in Vietnam could speak some English and were aware of what was going on in the area.

"Where you go in Phuoc Hai?" the driver asked.

"I don't know the street address. I'm looking for a young woman by the name of Lan. She once worked here at the hotel and restaurant. Did you ever take her home from the hotel?"

The driver was silent for a moment. "Lan, ya Lan. I never take her home. My friend, he always take her. Long time no see Lan. She no work at hotel now."

"Where is your friend? Is he at the hotel today?"

"No, my friend not work today. He now only work three day a week. Maybe tomorrow he be at hotel. I tell him you look for him, okay? You still like to go to Phuoc Hai?"

"Yeah, just drive me around Phuoc Hai. I want to look it over."

"Ya, okay, boss."

Phuoc Hai was certainly not the elite area of Nha Trang. Many of the thousands of refugees from the provinces north of Nha Trang had settled there. Dozens of small stores, barbershops, kiosks, beauty salons, hardware stores, cafes, coffee shops, and textile stores crowded the streets. Only the large thoroughfare that ran through the heart of the community was paved.

Several churches lined the main street. John noticed a large Catholic Church and two Protestant churches. The closer you came to the airport, the shabbier the houses became. In general, Phuoc Hai was a rather squalid community.

John had seen enough. "I want to go back to the hotel."

"Ya, boss."

Back in his room, John stretched across the bed. He felt drained and disappointed. He envisioned meeting Mai at the hotel and seeing the surprised look on her face. Thinking about Mai, John dozed off and dreamed he found her working in the field. She looked up and saw him coming and ran to him. She was so beautiful with her long, black hair streaming behind her. He reached out to embrace her…

John woke with a start and sat on the edge of the bed. He looked at his watch. It was 2:30 p.m. He felt disgusted for not getting up sooner. After washing his face, he went down to the restaurant and ordered a fried rice dish with a cup of coffee.

Unsure what to do with the rest of his afternoon, John ventured out of the hotel.

John wandered downtown, stopping to look over the goods at several kiosks on the streets. When he served in Nha Trang in 1972, street kiosks sold a wide assortment of goods that would appeal to American troops. Everything from cans of Coke, pocketknives, cigarette lighters, pocketbooks, caps and scarves, and cans of army rations could be bought at these booths. John found that the local market place and street vendors all over the city still carried these goods, although the Americans had been gone since 1973.

He walked toward the beach. When stationed in Nha Trang, he enjoyed the many restaurants on the beach. He would sit outside drinking coffee or a fruit drink and look out over the tranquil South China Sea with its small islands jutting out from the water in the near distance.

Several blocks from the beach he saw another foreigner walking toward him.

"Hello," the man said. "I don't see many Westerners in Nha Trang these days. Are you working here?"

"I'm just visiting. I was stationed here in the army back in '72 and '73. I know not many GIs come back to 'Nam, but I have a reason."

The man flashed a smile and held out his hand. "Hey, I'm Jeff Burt. It's nice to meet you. And I'm glad you came back to 'Nam. I think I've heard my friend Ted Danner mention you. Are you John Gunter?"

"Yeah, I am. I'd sure like to see Ted. I wrote him some time ago. Is he still in Nha Trang?"

"Ted's in Saigon for a conference this week. He'll be disappointed he missed you."

John asked, "What are you doing here in Nha Trang?"

"My family and I live here. We work with the churches in this area."

"You're missionaries?"

"Yes, we are. We've lived here since 1969.

"Your wife and children are here with you?"

"Yes, we live on Le Dai Hanh Street. You're welcome to visit us. Say, I'm curious. You said you came back for a reason?"

"Yeah, I came back to ... well—I came back to find the girl I met here. I want to marry her and take her back to the States. I met her at the Vien Dong Hotel where she worked as a cashier and hostess. She's not like other girls who worked there. She's different. She's a Christian. She went to the Protestant church downtown."

"Have you located her yet?"

"I just arrived yesterday and went to the Vien Dong, but she's not working there anymore. They said she went back to her village near Dalat. Tomorrow I'm gonna try to find a friend of hers that lives in Phouc Hai. This friend will know where her village is located. Her father has a farm where he grows fruits and vegetables."

"Good. I hope you find her. If I can be of any help, let me know. How about having dinner with us this evening about seven? Are you free?"

"Yeah, I can come. What's your address?"

"Number six Le Dai Hanh. Do you need a ride?"

"No, I'll take a taxi. But after dinner, you can take me back to the hotel if you don't mind."

"Sure. Let me write my address down for you. Just give it to the taxi. We'll see you then."

After several hours on the beach relaxing and sipping cold fruit drinks, John returned to the hotel, showered, and dressed for his dinner date with the Burts. He got a taxi and arrived at the Burts' a few minutes before seven.

Jeff greeted him at the gate. "Come on in. John, this is my wife, Ann, and these two bight-eyed kiddos are Josh and Marie. And John, this is Captain Thong and his wife, Brenda. They're having dinner with us also. Captain Thong is the Commanding Officer of the Intelligence Division of Khanh Hoa Province. We're members of the same church. Brenda grew up in San Antonio. She met Captain Thong two years ago at Fort Sam Houston where he came for training."

The couples sat down on sofas in the expansive living room/dining room. An overhead ceiling fan kept the warm air moving. The light pumpkin-colored tile floor gave the room a Florida look.

Jeff and Ann Burt were in their mid-thirties. Jeff grew up on a farm in East Texas and Ann on a farm in West Tennessee. They both felt God's call to be foreign missionaries and met at a seminary in Texas. Their two children had been still in diapers when they first arrived in Vietnam.

John was amazed at finding an American missionary family living in Vietnam. He said, "I can't believe you live here with your children. I was here a year and didn't know there were this many missionaries in 'Nam."

"Well, I guess we traveled in different circles," Jeff said. "There are more than a hundred missionaries from different churches living and working in South Vietnam."

"That many? That's incredible! Aren't you afraid to live here with all the fighting going on?"

"Actually, we live normal lives. We stay busy working with the churches during the day, and our children attend a school sponsored by a mission. In the evenings, we teach English classes to students, entertain friends, or go out to one of the restaurants for dinner. Yeah, we live normal lives here."

John listened but was incredulous. "I don't think I could take my children to Vietnam. It's a war zone."

Ann interrupted the conversation to announce that it was time to eat dinner. The three couples, along with Josh and Marie, were seated at the round dining table. Ann's southern fried chicken, creamed potatoes, peas, and hot rolls graced the table. Jeff blessed the food and prayed for their guests.

"Thanks for the prayer," John said. "Please remember me tomorrow that I might find out where Mai lives. I've got thirty-eight more days in 'Nam before I have to get back to the States. I don't want to waste a lot of time looking for Mai's village."

"Only thirty-eight days?" Ann asked. "You'll have to make every one count."

Jeff cautioned, "John, you need to move out on finding Mai and begin the process of getting her out of the country. The security situation here has broken down since the American pullout."

"Is it that bad? Nha Trang and this area were secure when I was here."

Captain Thong said, "John, things have changed since you left in seventy-three. The North Vietnamese Army is building up for something big. We don't know what they're planning, but we're concerned. The Communists already control the province west of Saigon. We think they're getting ready to launch a major offensive."

"Is it that serious? I've heard nothing about this build-up in the states."

"Vietnam is off the radar back in the good old USA. As far as the US is concerned, the war's over," Jeff said.

John stood and excused himself. "Thanks for the meal and your prayers."

"If I were you," Jeff advised, "I would ask Mai's friend to take you to her village. It might save you a lot of time and trouble.

Sometimes directions given cross-culturally are not the best. Here's our phone number. Give us a call if we can be of any help."

"Thanks. I'll do that."

"Come on, John. I'm going to give you a lift back to your hotel."

Back at the hotel, John felt good about his evening with the Burts. Their friendly and positive spirit encouraged him, and their advice would be helpful in his finding Mai.

5

March 2, Dalat and Lien

When John went down for breakfast, the taxi driver who knew Lan was already waiting for him. The taxi drivers, along with the rest of the city's economy, missed the presence of the American military.

After ordering his breakfast, he talked to the driver. "You know where Lan lives in Phouc Hai?"

The taxi driver was short and heavyset for a Vietnamese. His large, round face and benevolent smile reminded John of his favorite uncle. "Ya, I know where Lan lives. I'll take you there, all right?"

"Okay, but I want to eat breakfast first. You want to eat breakfast?"

"No, thank you. I ate early this morning."

"You speak English well."

"Ya, not so good. When the Americans were here, I worked as an interpreter at the army base. Then I made very good money. Now I just try to keep some simple food on the table."

After eating his eggs and rice, John gulped down his coffee and then followed the driver to the cab. He sat in the front seat so he could talk to the driver. "What is your name?"

"When I worked at the army base, they called me Sam. Sam's a good American name, isn't it?"

"Yeah, it is. You call me John. That's another good American name."

Coming to Phuoc Hai, Sam crossed several streets and stopped in front of a small house with a porch and white shutters that stood out in sharp contrast to the dark gray of the house. Various flowers and plants embellished the neat yard. Getting out of the cab, Sam said, "You wait here for a minute."

Sam knocked on the door and then turned and smiled at John as if to say everything would be okay. An older woman cautiously opened the door to greet Sam. They conversed for five minutes or more while John waited anxiously in the taxi.

When the driver returned, John asked, "What did she say, Sam?"

"So sorry because Lan is not here. She went to visit her cousin in Dalat."

"Does her mother know where the cousin lives in Dalat?"

"In the western part near a national police station."

"Do you think we can find her?"

"You want me to go with you to Dalat?"

"Yeah, Sam, I'd like you to take me to Dalat and help me find Lan. You know her better than I do. I'll pay you for the trip and take care of your expenses. Is that okay?"

"You mean you want me to take you to Dalat to look for Lan? We don't know where she is. It may take days. When do you want to go?"

"Today! Can you take me this morning?"

"You mean now? Now?"

"Yes, I want you to take me now. I can go by the hotel and get my suitcase."

"You Americans are all alike," Sam said. "You want things to happen now. Yes, I'll take you, John. When we go by the hotel, I'll send word to my wife. Maybe we can find Lan."

John said, "Lan is the key to finding Mai. she went with Mai once to visit her family on the farm, so I believe she will know exactly the way to her house."

Sam told John that Lan grew up in Nha Trang where her family owned and operated a large clothing store. While a student, she worked part-time in her parent's store. Her father died a year after she graduated from high school. Since her mother was unable to continue the business without her husband, Lan went job-hunting to help the family financially.

She was hired as cashier for the Vien Dong Hotel in downtown Nha Trang. With her experience working in the family store and her ability to relate to others, she functioned as business manager for the hotel. In that capacity, she met Mai and gave her a job as assistant cashier. She trained Mai, and in the process, they became good friends.

Sam said, "After the Americans left Vietnam in March 1973, business at the hotel dropped The hotel owners replaced Lan with one of their family members. She could not find a regular job but worked part time as she had opportunity.

John became acquainted with Lan when he came to the hotel restaurant once or twice weekly to see Mai. He remembered that Mai told him that Lan liked him and supported her dating him.

On the way up to Dalat, John took in the beauty of the alpine landscape of pine forests, rolling hills, and small lakes. He could feel the air becoming cooler as they neared Dalat.

When they arrived in the city, John was surprised at the large French-style villas. He remembered reading a book on the history of Vietnam and how the French colonized it from the middle of the nineteenth century until 1954. Dalat was their favorite resort city. They came to Dalat to escape the heat of Saigon and other southern cities.

"Do you know a good place to eat?" John asked Sam.

"Ya, there's a nice restaurant on the lake. We can eat and have a good view of the most famous lake in Vietnam, *Xuan Huong.*"

"What does 'Swan Who-on' mean?"

"The lake was named after one of our famous poets, Ho Xuan Huong."

The lake came into view right in the middle of the city. John was amazed at the beauty and tranquility of the scene. The restaurant Sam suggested was just off the road parallel to the lake.

After lunch on the lake, Sam said, "I have a brother who lives here. I'll stay with him and check you into a hostel. You may want to walk around and see the market and downtown Dalat."

At the hostel, John was pleased that the front desk clerk spoke English well.

"You don't need me here, John," Sam said. "This is a good place for you to stay. I'll see you in the morning about eight o'clock, okay?"

John climbed the stairs to his second-floor room and lay across the bed. Jet lag still had a hold on his body, and in two minutes he was sound asleep.

After waking up at four in the afternoon, John walked down to the lake and got a cup of coffee at one of the outdoor cafés. He walked to the Dalat Market. He thought he might see Mai there. After all, her family sold produce. Amazed at the freshness and size of the fruit, he bought a sack to take to his room.

As he left the market, he noticed a girl ahead of him with long, black hair about the same height and shape as Mai. Could it be? His chest tightened, and his heart pounded. He quickened his pace to catch a glimpse of her face under the conical straw hat. But when he came alongside her, it was not Mai.

Sam arrived at eight o'clock in the morning. John finished his coffee and French bread in the hostel lobby. "Sam, where and how are we going to start to find Lan?"

"We'll go to the western part of the city and look for a national police station. Then we will start asking in the neighborhood in that area."

"Sounds good to me."

In the western part of the city, they found the national police station. Sam drove a block beyond the station and parked his taxi at a neighborhood kiosk. John let Sam, the Vietnamese speaker, do the talking. "Do you know a woman in her middle twenties by the name of Lan? She's visiting a friend in this neighborhood."

No one seemed to know Lan or her cousin. After forty minutes of contacting people around that kiosk, they moved to one in another block. Sam talked to more than twenty people but with the same result.

"John, we have a problem. Lan is from Nha Trang, and nobody here knows her. And we don't know the name of her cousin or what she looks like. How are we going to find her?"

"I don't know, but I know if we don't find her, we can't find Mai. Lan is the only person I know who can take us to Mai's house. If we don't find Lan, my coming back to Vietnam is a waste of time and effort."

"It would be difficult to find Lan," Sam said, "even if we knew her neighborhood. How can we find her in the western part of the city? Thousands of people live in the western part of Dalat."

John looked at Sam and shrugged. "Then what's next, Sam? There must be some way we can find Lan."

"Don't give up. I want to try one more thing. Who knows? It may take another day or two, but we will find her."

John had his doubts, but he was willing to try whatever Sam suggested.

Early the next morning, Sam met John at the hostel on the lake.

"John, I have an idea. Let's go back to the same streets and go wherever they're selling *pho*. Most everyone comes out in the morning to get a bowl for breakfast. They sell it at the kiosks, and a mobile seller goes up and down the streets."

At the first kiosk, Sam ate a bowl of *pho* as they looked over the people from the nearby houses coming to get their breakfast. John watched Sam eat his *pho* soup with chopsticks and marveled at how skillfully he pushed the noodles into his mouth with a sucking noise. Sam wiped his mouth with the back of his hand and smacked his lips in satisfaction.

"John, let's go to the next street."

While they walked, they passed a mobile *pho* salesman with his container of hot broth, bottles of hot sauce, catsup, and onions on a two-wheeled push-cart. Every few steps he gave his melancholy call: "*Pho-o-o-o-o-o.*"

Just as they passed the salesman, they met a young woman walking toward the *pho* cart. The light of recognition broke on the face of the three simultaneously. "Lan!"

"Sam, John, is it you?"

"Lan, we've been looking all over for you," John said. "This is incredible!"

"Sam, John, how did you know where to find me?"

"We went to your mother's house in Phuoc Hai," Sam said. "She told us you lived in this part of town. She did not know the address, so we searched for you. We were lucky to meet you."

"John, Mai will be happy to see you. She missed you. She did not know you come back to Vietnam. She lives not so far from Dalat."

"Lan, I want to see Mai. Can you take us to her home village?"

"You mean now?"

"Yes, as soon as you can, Lan. My time in Vietnam is short."

"Yes, I can take you. Sam, my cousin's house has brown shutters, and the number is three-one-six. You see the house from here. Come at ten o'clock, and we will go to Lien to meet Mai, okay?"

"Okay, we will see you at ten o'clock. John, let us go by the hostel and pick up your suitcase."

6

At ten o'clock, they met Lan and drove down from Dalat toward Lien, a small town located near the local airport. Lan pointed to the road sign. "John, Mai's father's farm is three kilometers south of Lien just near the road to Saigon. You will soon see Mai."

John was silent with his thoughts. How would she receive him? Why had she not written? Did she now have another man in her life?

Lan seemed to know what John was thinking. "John, you do not worry. Mai still likes you. But you must go slowly. Mai's papa and mama have Vietnamese customs. They are not like people in downtown Nha Trang."

"I understand, Lan. Thank you for your advice. I want her family to like me. I will try to fit into their ways of doing things."

Two kilometers from town, Lan began to look intently out the car window to the left of the highway. "Sam, you go slow, okay? Mai's place near."

After another kilometer, Lan said, "Here, Sam. Turn here."

A house sat fifty meters from the highway with a barn-like building in back of it. Fruit orchards covered the land behind the barn.

Open vegetable gardens flourished alongside the fruit orchards. As they drove slowly down the dirt road that took them to the front of the house, John could see people working out behind the barn.

Sam parked in front of the house. They got out and waited to see who would come to greet them. No one appeared. Sam sized up the situation.

"The family is working behind the barn. I saw people moving around there when we pulled into the yard."

Walking toward the barn, John's heart pounded. After almost two years, he was going to see Mai again. His throat felt constricted and dry. Sweat popped out on his forehead.

They neared a group of people bent over, preparing the soil for planting. An older man and woman glanced up. They were startled to see strangers, one of them a foreigner. Seeing how frightened they were, Lan quickly called, "*Chao Thua Ong, Ba.* (Greetings, Sir and Mrs.)"

The entire group turned and looked at them. At first glance, John couldn't tell which figure was Mai. All the women wore long black pants, knit sweaters, and conical straw hats. One stood from her kneeling position and rushed toward Lan. Mai. The two women embraced and talked excitedly. Lan and Mai turned toward John.

"Mai," Lan explained, "John has come back to Vietnam to see you. I brought him here."

Mai's face flushed as she stepped toward John. "I'm happy to see you, John. You were gone a long time."

John reached out and took Mai's hand and squeezed it for a moment. Mai took off her conical hat. John studied her face. She was more beautiful than he remembered. Her black hair hung beyond her shoulders framing her sun-tanned, dimpled face and white teeth.

"Mai, I'm happy to see you again." John spoke slowly. "I've never forgotten you. I've thought about you every day since I left Vietnam."

Lan, sensitive that Mai's parents did not know the situation, introduced them to John and Sam. Then Mai introduced her two younger sisters and two younger brothers. Mai's parents invited Lan, Sam, and John into the house for tea. John followed Lan and Sam.

"This is very good," Sam told John. "It is good for us to sit and have tea with the family. You will need to have tea and talk with them often. They will study you and try to get to know you. Ya, I know you cannot speak Vietnamese, but Mai can interpret for you. In this way, she will review her English and get to know you again. She can interpret more than your words to her family. She can interpret you to them."

"Thanks, Sam. You've helped me a lot. When are you going back to Nha Trang?"

"When we finish our visit, I will excuse myself and return to Nha Trang."

After they were seated, John noticed that Mai was not seated with them. She was serving them. He could not keep his eyes off her. She was so beautiful.

"Sam," John whispered, "finding Mai has made me happier than I've been in a long time. Yet I'm a bit concerned about ... about how I'm going to talk to her family. The culture here is so different, and you won't be here to help me."

"No need to worry, John. You will do okay. Lan and Mai both will help you."

"It will be the greatest challenge of my life."

John did not know just how complex and dangerous the challenge would prove to be.

March 3, Lien

Before he returned to Nha Trang, Sam remembered that John would need a place to stay. He asked Mr. Tuan, Mai's father, "Sir, where can John stay in Lien?"

"He can stay at my sister's bed and breakfast place," Mr. Tuan said. "She is a widow whose husband was killed in battle fighting with the South Vietnamese Army. "When we drove through Lien, I saw a nice inn just off the Saigon highway. Was that your sister's?"

"Ya, that is her inn. In order to provide for her three children, she bought a large house in the middle of town and spent weeks renovating it. The inn serves breakfast and has six small bedrooms for overnight guests."

Sam took John to Mr. Tuan's sister's inn and introduced him to Mrs. Dao. Truck and bus drivers and tourists patronized the neat, thriving inn, and many of the locals took advantage of its delicious breakfast. Mrs. Dao spoke only a few words of English, so the conversation was in Vietnamese.

John noticed how Mai resembled her aunt. In her mid-forties, Mrs. Dao's fair complexion complimented her dark eyes and hair.

After talking with Mrs. Dao, Sam explained to John, "You pay three dollars a day for your bed and breakfast, okay?"

"Thanks, Sam. Thanks for all your help," John said. "I hope to see you sometime in Nha Trang. You have a good trip back down the mountain."

John followed Mrs. Dao's youngest son, fifteen-year-old Hien, to a small room where he would sleep. Hien set down John's suitcase and smiled at him. "You teach me some English, okay? I study English in school. You call me Harry."

"Harry." John held out his hand. "You can call me John. I am happy to be your friend. Can you help me buy a bicycle?"

Seeing the puzzled look on Harry's face, John acted out riding a bicycle. He could see the light of understanding break on Harry's face. "John want to buy a *xe dap*—a bysil. Okay, Harry help John buy a bysil."

"Harry, you can call it a bike, okay?"

"Ya, okay, John, a bike."

John had thought about the three kilometers to the Tuan's farm and knew a bicycle would be a good way to get around the area.

7

The following morning before breakfast, Harry knocked on John's door and motioned for him to come outside. "You see. Good *xe dap*. Good bike, okay?"

A young man stood beside a bicycle. "You give ten American dollars," Harry said.

John paid the man and went to park the bicycle beside the inn. "No, John," Harry said, "no can put bike outside. John must put in room. Bad people steal John's bike."

Although he felt clumsy in doing so, John pushed the bicycle into his room and parked it at the head of his bed. After all, he could hang his clothes on it at night.

Mrs. Dao's breakfast was the best in town. That was evident by the fact that the fifteen-seat table was full each morning. At least half the people were local businessmen. John enjoyed the boiled eggs, French bread with butter, and fruit. The locally grown coffee was delicious. The Vietnamese guests were happy to have John at the table. They were curious to know about him.

"Hello, my name is Hao," said the man next to him in excellent English. "You can call me Hal. That's my American name. I stayed in America for one year training as a helicopter pilot in Mineral Wells, Texas."

"I'm happy to meet you, Hal. My name is John. I'm from Hopewell, Texas, which is near Mineral Wells. Are you still in the army?"

"No, I received a medical discharge after twelve years of service. I am now a businessman."

"What kind of business are you in?"

"I have a fleet of taxis and a trucking company. My taxis meet tourists at the airport and take them to other places in this area. My seven trucks haul for the government and for private companies. Most of my drivers are veterans." Hal paused. "What kind of business are you in? Are you here with the American government?"

"No, I'm a tourist. I served a year here in the army, and I've come back to visit a friend."

Hal translated the conversation to the Vietnamese guests. They smiled their approval at John's coming back to visit their country.

After all the guests had dismissed themselves with polite nods and smiles, Hal remained with John at the table. He was eager to get better acquainted with his American friend. They talked about life in the small towns of West Texas. Finally, Hal rose to leave.

"John, if you need a taxi, you let me know, okay?"

"Thanks, Hal," John replied. "I'll probably need one from time to time."

"John, I'm very happy that you've come here. I will be your friend." Before he went out the door, Hal looked back. "John, you must be careful. The Viet Cong are probing and attacking our militia forces several nights a week. Something is going on. You must not go out at night because it is not safe now."

Back in his room, John thought about Hal's comments, and he remembered what Jeff Burt had told him about the buildup of Communist forces in South Vietnam. He must move forward with his plan to get Mai out. In months to come, this country could fall to the Communists. Then it might be too late.

At mid-morning John decided to go out to the Tuan farm to see Mai and to get better acquainted with the Tuan family.

He rode his new bicycle to the Tuan farm. Parking it beside the barn, he saw the family working in the field. Lan came to meet him. Lan decided to stay with Mai and her family for a while. She'd asked Sam to go by her cousin's house in Dalat and tell her she would be in Lien for a time.

"John, you come to work with us? You can work beside Mai and me. We'll show you how to plant *van-van.*" Seeing his puzzled look, Lan explained, "*Van-van* are vegetables—cabbage, okra, spinach, and turnip greens. This is the season for *van-van.*"

Mr. and Mrs. Tuan smiled at John and seemed pleased that he came to work with them. The younger brothers and sisters giggled and glanced toward John at every opportunity.

John had never worked in a garden, but he quickly saw how they were carefully preparing the earth. After the seeds were planted, one of the younger sisters came with a sprayer to give them just the right amount of water.

At noontime, women brought food out to the workers. One container was filled with steaming white rice, and another had cabbage mixed with meat. After everyone washed their hands in a tin basin, they sat in a circle around the food. Mr. Tuan blessed it with prayer.

The children could not suppress their laughter as they watched John try to master the use of chopsticks. Finally, in desperation, he said, "Mai, show me how to use chopsticks. You all make it look so easy. There must be a trick to it."

"Let the chopsticks rest on your middle finger, like this. Use your forefinger to guide them, okay?"

After several minutes of practice, John improved somewhat. But Lan, Mr. and Mrs. Tuan, and even Mai failed to hide their mirth behind shy smiles. John didn't mind. He enjoyed getting to know Mai's family.

When all the seeds were planted, John, Mai, and Lan sat under a large tree and talked. John told about his time back in the States with his family.

"Now, tell me about your time after I left Nha Trang," John said.

Mai blushed as she told about coming back to the farm and getting back into the life of her community. She told about her church and how happy she was to worship again with family and friends. Their pastor had been a great encouragement. He attended the seminary in Nha Trang where he learned under several professors from America. He studied English also in a class taught by the wife of one of the American professors.

Mai paused. "John, you can go to church with us and meet Pastor Chanh. He is a good man. You will like him. He speaks good English."

As she talked, John felt peace fill his heart and mind. The late evening shadows were lengthening. A bird chirped, and the sun began its descent behind the mountains. John thought, *I could stay here with Mai forever.* But Mai brought John out of his reverie.

"You must go now. It is not good to go in the dark."

Having observed that in the Vietnamese culture it was customary to ask permission to be dismissed, John addressed Mr. and Mrs. Tuan. Then he pedaled furiously to get to his room before dark.

When he arrived at the inn, Harry was waiting for him. "You go with Harry," he said. "I show you cafe to eat, okay? We eat; we talk English, okay?"

Harry took John to a small roadside cafe fifty meters from the inn. While eating a plate of fried rice, John helped Harry with his English. Though he was tired, he admired Harry's enthusiasm and desire to learn English.

When they returned to the inn, Harry said, "John, I show you. You follow Harry." At the back part of the inn, Harry knelt on the floor and pushed back a small rug. Grasping a small bent nail, he pulled up a hidden door in the floor. With a flashlight, he motioned for John to follow him down some steps. They stood in a small room.

"Sometimes VC come," Harry explained. "We hide. They no find, okay?"

The dank smell of the seldom-used space stung John's nostrils. A spider web blanketed the top right corner. The secret room measured eight feet wide, six feet high, and eight feet long. Rough wooden planks gave the walls a barn-like appearance. A straw mat served as a rug.

Later on that night, muffled explosions of mortars falling nearby awakened John. From the sound, he projected the location to be the national police station located just off the highway north of the inn. After several minutes of staccato chatter from M-16s, silence followed. John knew if anything serious happened, Harry would tell him. Sooner or later, he knew he would have to use the secret room.

8

March 5, 1975

At breakfast, John noticed a young man sitting across from him. In contrast to the friendly faces of the other guests, a scowl creased the face of this man. John glanced toward him several times and caught him looking his way with an angry frown. When all the other guests left the table, John remained to talk with Hal.

"Hal, who was the young man sitting across the table from me?"

"That was Minh. He drives one of my trucks. I hired him because I could get no one else. I don't like him or trust him, but I need him to drive my truck."

"He kept glancing at me as if he didn't like me. He looked hostile."

"I'm not surprised. He doesn't like Americans. When he was a boy, his father was killed by the late President Diem's secret police. His family believes the Americans had something to do with it. His father was a local political figure and strongly opposed President Diem." After a moment of thought, Hal added, "The Americans would have no interest in a local politician."

"Where does he live?"

"He lives with his mother on a large piece of land near Mr. Tuan's farm. His mother has several vegetable gardens. She sells her produce at the local market, but Minh doesn't like to work on the farm. He drives a truck for me to make his own money. By the way, he likes Mr. Tuan's daughter, Mai. He went to school with her, and it's no secret he would like to marry her." Hal paused. "You like Mai also, don't you? Someone told me you spent the day with her family yesterday."

"That's true. I met Mai in Nha Trang when I was in the army. I love her, and I want to marry her and take her back to America. That's why I came here."

Hal was quiet for a few moments. "You must be very careful. Minh is a dangerous person. I've seen his anger explode several times. This is a dangerous situation for you. Minh hates Americans, and you are here in his hometown wanting to marry the girl he loves."

"Thanks for the warning. I'll keep my eyes open."

After breakfast, John went out to the farm to work in the field with Mai and her family. He enjoyed the outdoors and being close to the earth. As a city boy back in Texas, he often wanted to live in the country. He envied his classmates who lived on farms and ranches.

The opportunity to work beside Mai made his time in the field special. They laughed and talked as people do when they're in love. She told him about the planting and harvesting of vegetables and fruits, the customs of Vietnamese farmers, and the legends that permeated Vietnamese culture.

At lunchtime, Mai's siblings came home from school and later joined them working in the field. Around four thirty, the family stopped their work and walked toward the barn.

"I'll make you a kite like the kind we make in America," John told Mai's siblings.

They rushed ahead of John and Mai to prepare the needed materials. On a worktable behind the barn, they launched into their kite construction project. John had made many for his younger brother, so it didn't take long.

In the open field, to the delight of the children, a strong breeze blowing in from the mountain soon had it airborne. John was so caught up in flying the kite with the children that he paid no attention to the setting sun. Mai realized it was getting late.

"John, you must hurry back before dark."

After he dismissed himself, John pedaled vigorously. Darkness was about to close in on him, but he felt pleased with the day on the farm. It was good to get away from talk about the war and the tensions associated with it. He felt refreshed and assured of his love for Mai.

As he rode along deep in his thoughts, he did not notice the truck until it was twenty yards behind him. He glanced back and saw it veering toward him without checking its speed. Instinctively he whipped the bicycle off the tarmac to the dirt shoulder of the highway. The quick reaction saved him. The truck barely missed him. John struggled to get control of his bicycle. He did not get a good look at the driver as the truck roared off in the dusk.

In the wash of emotions that followed the close call with death, he remembered Hal telling him Minh was one of his truck drivers. In that moment, he knew the driver was Minh and that Minh would try again to kill him.

He pedaled back to the inn, entered through the side door, and pushed the bicycle toward his room. Harry stopped him.

"John, you gone all day. Harry no can practice English with you. Harry your friend, okay?"

Harry's friendly gesture released a warm feeling in John. "Thanks, Harry. Tomorrow I'll practice English with you. Now I'm tired. I'm going to my room."

John sat on the bed and tried to recall all that happened to him that day. His mind and body were so tired he didn't want to go over his close brush with death. He lay back and was soon sound asleep.

The attack by the VC on Lien and the battle with the local militia at midnight did not disturb John. But most of the residents slept fitfully, wondering what lay ahead for them.

John placed a call to the Burts in Nha Trang at the Lien post office. Ann answered the phone. "Ann, John Gunter here. I'm in the town of Lien near the Dalat airport. I found Mai, and I'm staying in an inn three kilometers from her house. Thanks for the dinner and time with your family and friends."

"Great to hear from you, John. I'm happy that you found Mai, and we'll look forward to meeting her. We enjoyed meeting you and having you as our guest. Captain Thong, you know our friend that you met here, is going to Dalat and on to Bien Hoa in a few days. I'm sure he's going through Lien. I'll mention to him that you're staying at Lien. Where is the inn located, John?"

"The inn is on the main highway going through Lien. Tell Captain Thong to drop by and have a cup of coffee with me."

Three days later, Captain Thong showed up for breakfast at the inn. He was accompanied by a lieutenant and a sergeant. "John, we stayed in Dalat last night, but we heard about the good breakfast here. It's good to meet you again. Ann and Jeff told me you were in Lien."

"It's a pleasure to meet you again, Captain."

Tall, with a lithe, wiry build, Captain Thong exuded a quiet confidence and a commanding presence.

While they were eating and talking, Dao came in to replenish the breakfast table. Captain Thong rose to his feet. "Dao, how are you? I haven't seen you in a while. Is this your inn?"

Dao and Captain Thong carried on an animated conversation for some minutes. After she returned to the kitchen, he said to his men and John, "Dao's husband and I were the best of friends. He was killed more than two years ago near Pleiku. He was a good officer…one of the best."

After breakfast, Captain Thong asked, "John, what are your plans? I heard that you want to marry Dao's niece as soon as possible and return to the states."

"Yeah, that's what I'd like to do, but I think it going to take more time than I thought."

"John, everything here goes slower than in America. You'll need to be patient, but you need to move out as quickly as possible. Every day it's getting more insecure."

"Do you think there's going to be a major offensive?"

"We're hearing that there's a lot of activity along the Cambodian border. This could indicate a build-up for an all out push into South Vietnam."

"Captain, when do you think this will happen?"

"It could happen any time. I'm concerned for our country."

"John, we've got to go. If I can help you in any way, get in touch with me. The Burts know how to contact me."

Captain Thong, with his fellow soldiers, climbed into their jeep and sped off toward Bien Hoa. Standing watching the jeep speed down the highway, John knew that he had been warned to get on with his efforts to marry Mai and get her out of the country.

9

March 10, Lien and Dalat

After breakfast at the inn, John said, "Hal, you mentioned I could use one of your taxis?"

"Ya, John, when do you want to use it?"

"Tomorrow. I want to take Mai to Dalat for an all-day outing. She can show me around the city, and we can eat in a good restaurant. I think it will be good for us if we can get away from the farm for a while."

"Good idea. Dalat is a romantic city. You know it's called the 'honeymoon city,' don't you?"

"Yeah, I've heard that."

"I'll have a taxi here early tomorrow morning. You can use it all day. No problem."

"Thanks, Hal. I appreciate it, and I'll drive carefully."

Later that morning John went out to the farm and talked to Mai and Lan about going to Dalat. John knew Mai's parents would be more open to her going with him, if Lan accompanied them. Mai and Lan danced like young schoolgirls at the possibility of an outing.

With Lan as interpreter, John asked Mr. Tuan for permission to take Mai and Lan to Dalat. He agreed and seemed pleased that Lan would go with them.

John woke early the next morning and hurried into the kitchen. Harry greeted him. "John, you get bread, cheese, coffee, okay? Here, Hal give me keys for taxi. You drive safe. Have good day."

At the farm, Mai and Lan met him in front of the house. "John, we're ready to go." Mai could barely contain her excitement. "I could hardly sleep last night. We're going to have a great time, aren't we?"

The threesome drove to Dalat chattering all the way. Mai talked about some places of interest they could see and a restaurant that served good food.

When they came into the city, John parked the taxi on a side street near the city center. They walked through the market selling vegetables, fruits, and flowers. Mai knew several of the women who worked there. Then they went down to the lake and ordered coffee at one of the outdoor cafes looking over the lake waters shimmering in the warm sunlight.

"John, look up the hill," Mai said. "That's the Dalat Palace Hotel. It was built by the French in the nineteen twenties. Many famous people have stayed in this hotel."

Lan added, "There's a nice view of the lake from the hotel. But only the rich can stay there. When we come to Dalat, most of us stay in hostels and small bed and breakfast places." She set her cup on the table and stood up. "Please excuse me. I want to visit my cousin. I'll meet you for lunch at the Can Tho Restaurant. See you then."

John noticed paddleboats on the lake and wanted to rent one. Mai smiled her pleasure at the idea. They paddled out toward the center of the lake. As they floated, John told Mai about life in America and about his work with the trucking company.

John realized his time with Mai was short. He decided to act.

"Mai, I've got twenty-nine more days in Vietnam. In less than a month, I have a flight out of Saigon to America. I love you. I want to marry you and take you back to America with me. Mai, will you marry me?"

Mai blushed. She looked intently at John with a misty, wide-eyed look.

Not sure she understood, John blurted, "Mai, do you understand me? I love you and want to marry you and take you to America."

"Ya, I understand," Mai whispered. "I love you, John, and I'm very happy to marry you and go with you to America. Yes, I'm very happy."

John leaned toward Mai and kissed her cheek. Then he kissed the beautiful lips he had thought of and dreamed about for so long. Alone in the middle of the lake, he kissed her again and again.

Lan met them at the appointed time and place. She immediately noticed the radiant look on Mai's face and knew, with a woman's intuition, that something romantic happened on the lake. After they ordered, with a coy smile, Lan ventured, "John, you asked Mai to marry you?"

He blushed and smiled. "Yeah, I did, and she said yes. We're going to get married soon, and I'm taking her back to America with me. We're happy."

"I'm glad for you, Mai and John. You will have many children and live happy lives. Don't forget Lan in Vietnam, okay?"

"Mai and I will not forget you, Lan. You must be in our wedding."

"Yes, I will be in your wedding." Lan smiled. "John, you must ask permission from Mr. Tuan to marry Mai. You must do this quickly. The war news is not good. I'm afraid for you and Mai. Move quickly, John."

On the way back to Lien, Lan said little. Finally, she told them, "I'm going back to Nha Trang tomorrow. My mama and family miss me and need me. I also miss them."

"Lan, you've been a great help to us," John said. "We'll miss you. I'll get a taxi to take you to Dalat. Then I'll take care of your bus fare to Nha Trang, okay?"

"Thank you, John. You're a good man. I'm happy for Mai."

Upon arriving back in Lien, they heard the news that Ban Me Thuot fell to the invading NVA forces. The news affected the general population. John could see worried looks and even fear on the faces of the people at the inn and about the town. They knew their nation was in crisis.

Later that evening, Hal came by the inn to get the taxi. Hal, usually jovial, had a worried look on his face. "John, things look bad for our country. I advise you to leave as soon as possible. It will become more dangerous every day."

"Thanks, Hal. I'll leave as soon as I can. Tomorrow I'm going to ask Mr. Tuan's permission to marry Mai. I want us to marry and leave for America."

"You must act quickly," Hal told him. "The time for us is getting short."

Time was even shorter for Lien than most of the population could have imagined.

10

March 11, Lien

John woke early and slipped on his clothes. Going to the kitchen he saw Mrs. Dao cooking breakfast. A fresh pot of coffee sent forth an enticing aroma to awaken the taste buds of coffee drinkers on the cool, clear morning.

Mrs. Dao poured John a generous cup and handed him a large piece of French bread with a chunk of cheese. He smiled at her kindness and nodded in appreciation. He chewed slowly as he thought about his plans for the day.

He pushed his bicycle out the side door of the inn and ride toward the Tuan farm. The taxi was coming for Lan at eight thirty. John needed to be at the farm by seven thirty so Lan could interpret this most important conversation for him.

When he arrived at the farm, the family was finishing their morning tea.

He asked Lan, "Would you interpret for me as I ask Mr. Tuan for permission to marry Mai? I think it's better for you to interpret rather than Mai."

"Ya, John, I will interpret for you. It is better for me to do it."

Lan spoke to Mr. and Mrs. Tuan and told them John wanted to talk to them about something important. After saying something to Lan, they walked into their guest room and arranged the chairs and tea table.

Lan explained to John that they were preparing for the meeting. "I did not tell them what you want to talk about, but I think they know you will talk to them about Mai. They're getting ready for an important meeting."

Mrs. Tuan instructed Mai to prepare refreshments; then she and Mr. Tuan went into their private room. Some minutes later, wearing their traditional Vietnamese clothing, they solemnly entered the guest room and sat down.

"John, we can go in now," Lan said.

Mai brought the refreshments and left the room.

Mr. and Mrs. Tuan invited everyone to drink tea and eat sweets. John had learned that in Vietnamese culture you wait until you're invited the second or third time before you eat or drink what is set before you. John watched Lan. After the third invitation, she reached for her tea. He followed her lead.

John could tell that Lan and Mai's parents were engaging in small talk. When Lan switched to a more serious tone, he knew she was telling Mai's parents why he wanted to meet with them. They frequently glanced toward him, saying, *"Vang,"* meaning "yes, I understand what you're saying," not necessarily, "yes, I agree with you."

Lan turned to John. "Now, John, you ask what you want, and I tell them, okay?"

John addressed them very carefully and deliberately. "I appreciate your gracious hospitality in the weeks I have visited your home. I have observed how you love and care for your children and have reared them to be honest, hardworking, and obedient. I know you are proud of Mai. She is a beautiful, obedient, and loving daughter."

Mr. and Mrs. Tuan nodded their heads with pleased expressions. John leaned forward toward them. "I love Mai, and I want to marry her. I will be a good husband to her and take care of her. I want to take her to America with me."

Lan interpreted all that John had said.

Mr. and Mrs. Tuan discussed between themselves for more than five minutes. Then they spoke to John through Lan. "Yes, we give you permission to marry our daughter. She loves you, and we think you are a good man. We have known that you love our daughter and want to marry her. We have already discussed it."

Mr. and Mrs. Tuan gestured with their hands for Lan and John to drink their tea and try the teacakes. Mr. Tuan took a bite of his teacake and chewed it slowly. "When do you want to marry our daughter?"

"I want to marry her soon because I need to return to America in twenty-two days."

"No, it is impossible for you to marry our daughter that soon," Mr. Tuan replied. "She will be married in the church, and we must have time to prepare for the wedding."

"When can we marry in the church?" John asked.

"We cannot answer you now. Later we will tell you the time that you can marry our daughter."

The taxi drove up to take Lan to Dalat. John politely dismissed himself and walked outside. Lan needed time to ask permission to leave and to say good-bye to Mai.

When Lan came out, John accompanied her to the taxi. He was concerned about the time of the wedding. He asked Lan, "Would you ask Mr. and Mrs. Tuan to set the wedding earlier? The war situation looks bad, and I need to leave the country in twenty-two days."

"John, I cannot do that. You talk to Pastor Chanh. Maybe he can help you."

Riding back to the inn, John thought about his dilemma. The country was in a critical situation. He must leave soon. Yet he would not leave without Mai.

John parked his bicycle at the door of the dining room. Mrs. Dao and Harry were still cleaning up from breakfast. He got another cup of Mrs. Dao's coffee and sat at an empty table. He must go to Pastor Chanh. Perhaps he could persuade Mr. Tuan to set an earlier date for the wedding. Pastor Chanh would understand the situation. There was no time to waste. He would go now.

The church and parsonage were located half a kilometer north of the center of Lien. John attended the church with Mai and her family. Pastor and Mrs. Chanh both spoke fluent English. They invited him to visit with them at any time.

John parked his bicycle in front of the church and knocked on the parsonage door. Mrs. Chanh greeted him. "Hello, John. Would you please come in?"

"Thank you. Is Pastor Chanh in today?"

"He is in his office at the church. I'll send one of the children to get him."

"No, please, I'll go to the church."

When John entered the church building, he saw Pastor Chanh in his small office at the back of the sanctuary. The pastor heard him enter and came out to meet him.

"John, how are you today? I'm very happy to see you again. Would you please come into my office?"

John sat in a chair across from the pastor's desk. They engaged in the formalities of light conversation. Then John came to the point of his visit. "Pastor, yesterday I asked Mai to marry me and go with me to America. She said yes, and I'm very happy about that."

"Congratulations, John. Have you asked the Tuans for permission to marry Mai?"

"That's what I want to talk to you about, Pastor." John sighed. "I did ask their permission this morning, and the Tuans gave their blessing. But they want a church wedding some time in the future."

"When does he want to have the wedding?"

"I don't know. He said he would tell me when the date was confirmed. I know it will be a month or more. With Ban Me Thuot falling, I don't know whether we have another month."

"I'm not sure either," replied Pastor Chanh. "The condition of the country is more critical than most people realize."

"Pastor, would you persuade Mr. Tuan to have the wedding earlier?"

"John, I know Mr. Tuan well. He is a good man, but I know I can't persuade him to change his mind about the wedding. He and his family have been through so many years living with war that they are hardened to it. I doubt if he knows anything about the present situation or even cares about it. Many Vietnamese ignore the war. That's their way of surviving."

"You mean he will go on planning for the wedding regardless of war conditions?"

"Yes, he will set a wedding date and plan for it, ignoring the war. Mr. Tuan and his family came to South Vietnam in 1954 when the French agreed to surrender North Vietnam to the Viet Minh, the Communists. More than nine hundred thousand Vietnamese chose not to live under Communism and moved south."

"I didn't know that. That's a large number of people."

"Yes, it is. Catholics composed about two-thirds of that number. The rest were former soldiers, policemen, and civil servants who had worked with the French. Many in that group were Protestants, including Mr. Tuan and his family. You see, John, they have been living with war for twenty-five years. You understand why they try to ignore it?"

"Yes, I understand more now. How about you, Pastor? Will you be safe if the Viet Cong and North Vietnamese launch an all-out attack on this area?"

"No. The Viet Cong have already tried to assassinate me. Two years ago I was ambushed and shot in the shoulder. I gave full throttle to my motorcycle and escaped. Just after arriving at my house, I fainted from loss of blood. Praise the Lord, I healed from my wound and have been going full-speed since my recovery."

"Have they tried to kill you since that time?"

"No, I have kept one step ahead of them. Montagnard Christians keep me informed about the activities of the Viet Cong. They have kept me from been ambushed again. I also exercise a holy caution in my ministry, but I'm ready to die."

"Why do the Viet Cong want to kill you?"

"I'm not sure, but I think it's because I help and encourage the Montagnard churches. Some of the Montagnards work with the Green Berets and CIA, so the VC really hate them. They identify me with them and also the Americans because I speak English and attended a seminary where there were several American professors."

"Pastor, your family and congregation need you alive. You must be careful."

"John, I'm going to carry out my ministry among my people. If the Communists capture this area, they'll probably kill me. If they do, I'll go to be with Jesus. They can't kill my soul, the real me."

"Pastor Chanh, I'm more challenged by your faith than by all the sermons and teachings I've heard in the past. Will you pray for me that I might do what God wants me to do regardless of what happens?"

"Yes, I have and will continue to pray for you, John."

Back in his room at the inn, John laid back on his bed looking at the ceiling. He knew he was in the most dangerous situation of his life. He considered his options. He could catch a bus or take a taxi to Saigon today, or he could wait and see how things developed.

If he knew when the highland area was going to be invaded by the Communists, he might have time to get out. But he would not leave without Mai. Somehow they would have time to marry and leave before conditions became too critical.

In a short time, John would have the opportunity to exercise the option he chose that day.

11

March 13, Lien

"Hien, it's time for you to take your Aunt Hai her food package and medicine," Mrs. Dao reminded her son. Harry (Hien) took his Aunt Hai a package once a week without fail. For Harry, it was no chore, for he actually enjoyed his time with Aunt Hai. She always had something for him to eat. She made him feel special, and he enjoyed every minute.

As they drank tea and ate sweet rice rolls, Aunt Hai told him stories about his dad when they were growing up together. She was the older sister. Harry never grew tired of hearing about his dad. He was devastated when he heard the news that he was killed in battle. He missed him very much.

Aunt Hai's husband had died this past year. Mrs. Dao invited her to come and live with them at the inn, but she refused. "This is my little spot in the world," she said. "I know everything about it. I've spent twenty years here. I have my dogs, chickens, and garden. No, I won't move. I'll die here."

Once a week, Harry went to the only pharmacy in town and bought Aunt Hai's blood pressure medicine. They would sell only a week's supply. Then Harry bought her favorite rice cakes and candies. After taking the goodies home, his mother, Dao, would pack in cooked food Aunt Hai enjoyed.

So Harry's trip to visit Aunt Hai was important to her, to him, and to all the family. The extended family knew Aunt Hai was being taken care of, and this pleased them.

Harry told Aunt Hai about John and their friendship.

"Bring John with you next week," she told Harry. "I want to meet him."

After breakfast on Saturday morning, Harry invited John. "I go to Aunt Hai on Monday. You go with me, okay?"

"Okay, Harry, I'll go with you."

On Monday morning, Harry and John rode their bicycles to the Tuans and walked the two kilometers to Aunt Hai's house. Aunt Hai was excited about John's visit. Talking all the while, she put out her finest silverware and dishes. Harry tried desperately to interpret her animated chatter.

"Aunt Hai says welcome. She happy you come here. She honored you come to her house."

Harry usually visited with Aunt Hai until about an hour before sundown. But on this day, he and John stayed longer than usual. When they were ready to leave, Harry told John, "We must go fast."

After hugging his Aunt, Harry led John down the trail at a fast lope. If they didn't hurry, night would catch them. Around a bend in the trail they saw two men walking toward them. Harry could tell by their dress and automatic weapons they were Viet Cong.

He whispered, "VC, John, VC. Go with Harry!"

They turned off the trail into a thickly wooded area. After running two hundred meters, they stopped to listen for the sound of footsteps. Yes, the men were following them and were not far behind. They took off running again. This time they accelerated their speed.

Harry knew this area. He spent many hours playing in these woods with his friends between his Uncle Tuan's farm and Aunt Hai's house. He remembered a gully he used as a hiding place. It was near a small creek surrounded by ferns. When he lay in the gully, no one could see him. He motioned to John, veered off to his left, and headed for his favorite hiding place.

The two VC were forty meters behind them. They could not be easily shaken off the track. The VC were tough, well-trained men and knew how to move in the woods.

Both Harry and John were good runners and had stamina. With Harry leading the way, they had the advantage over the Viet Cong in that they knew exactly where they wanted to go. They stopped and listened. They could hear the pursuers moving rapidly through the woods.

John and Harry sprinted forward. They came to a dry creek bed. They raced down thirty meters and then turned left along a small running creek. Coming to Harry's secret gully, they jumped in and laid down, face up. Harry reached out with his pocketknife and cut several ferns to place over them. It would be difficult for anyone to see them.

Harry listened for footsteps. Yes, they were coming. Harry nudged John's foot and put a finger to his lips. He knew the consequences of being captured by the Viet Cong. Prisoners would submit and become one of them or be killed.

They could hear the VC coming nearer and nearer. The two stopped only a few meters from the gully. Could the enemy see them? They held their breath. After a minute that seemed like an eternity, the footsteps moved in another direction. But Harry did not move. He signaled John to stay down. He knew that one of the Viet Cong tricks was to pretend they were gone while waiting for their prey to show themselves. They would not fool Harry. Laying still in the gully, Harry and John dozed off to sleep.

John awoke with a start. At first, he couldn't remember where he was or why he was lying in a gully. He sat up and saw that Harry was with him. It was pitch dark. John listened for any sound of movement. Not hearing anything, he slowly stood up. He could hear Harry's deep breathing accompanied by the chirping of night insects.

Just as he was about to step out of the gully, he heard the sound of footsteps coming toward him. He squatted down again and then laid back in the gully. He could hear the muffled footsteps of five or six people on the trail running parallel with the creek. They passed ten meters from the gully.

John considered their position and plight. If they stayed in the gully until early morning, it would be safer than trying to walk out of the woods now. The place was crawling with Viet Cong.

John covered himself with fern branches and eventually fell asleep again.

At the inn, Hal went into the kitchen to check on John and Harry. He knew Harry's routine of going each week to visit his Aunt Hai's house. This concerned Hal, for he knew the increased level of Viet Cong activity around Lien in the past two weeks. Harry usually returned shortly before dark, but he and John were nowhere to be seen.

Hal asked Mrs. Dao, "Where are Harry and John?"

She shrugged her shoulders. "Harry should be here. He has never stayed out this late."

While Mrs. Dao moved about in the kitchen, Hal paced back and forth in the dining room. What could he do? It was dark, and going out would be dangerous.

"I'm going to the Tuans," Hal told Mrs. Dao. "Harry and John rode their bikes to the farm. Maybe the Tuans know something."

"Hal, isn't it dangerous for you to drive at night?"

"No, the Viet Cong also use my taxis. They never bother us."

Arriving at the Tuan house, he asked about John and Harry. No one has seen them since they left their bikes at the barn.

"Hal, I'm concerned about them," Mai said. "They should have returned before dark."

Hal knew Mrs. Dao was concerned also. "I need to go back to the inn. Mrs. Dao will be waiting to see if I have any news. Please excuse me."

When Hal arrived at the inn, Mrs. Dao was still working in the kitchen. He said, "Harry and John have not come back for their bicycles."

She began to cry. Hal tried to comfort and assure her. "They'll probably show up in the morning. Maybe they decided to spend the night."

"No, Harry would not do that without asking my permission." Mrs. Dao's voice choked with emotion.

That night no one in Harry's family slept soundly.

The early morning chirping of birds woke John and Harry. They pushed the ferns off and sat up. After listening to the sounds around them for several minutes, they got up and washed their faces in the nearby stream. The water was ice cold and drove the sleepiness out of them.

"Harry, do you think its okay to go now?"

"Ya, okay now. No VC in morning. Harry go fast. Mama look for me."

Harry and John trotted back to the Tuan's barn. Since it was dawn, the Tuan family was still asleep. Getting on their bikes, John and Harry pedaled back to the inn. They pushed their bikes in the side door. Harry could imagine the trauma their overnight disappearance caused his mother and others.

Hearing someone come in, Mrs. Dao glanced their way. It took a second for her to comprehend that it was Harry and John.

"Hien! Where have you been? Why have you stayed out all night like this? This is not the way you should treat your mother." Although she was chiding and rebuking him, Mrs. Dao could not hide her joy and tears at seeing him home safe.

"Mama, we had to hide in the woods all night because of the VC. There were many of them out last night. But it's no big thing. We slept well in a gully. We woke early, and here we are, ready for the day." Hien patted his mother's hand. "Mama, I'll tell you more later, but now we need to get breakfast ready for our guests."

12

Sunday, March 16

The church was packed for the worship service. People stood, filling the room, and more crowded outside trying to hear the message. John sat with the Tuan family. Although he could not understand the message, he sensed the emotion and intensity with which Pastor Chanh delivered it to the somber crowd.

The fact that their nation was in crisis was reflected on the faces of the congregation. Tears coursed down the cheeks of some of the women.

After the service, Pastor Chanh spoke to John. "The Communists attacked Pleiku and Kontum this morning. I heard it on the early news. If Pleiku and Kontum fall, the Communist forces will head for the coast. Every day the situation is becoming more dangerous. John, you need to think about your options."

"I have been considering them, Pastor."

"One more thing. Montagnard friends told me yesterday that Minh is a Viet Cong. He's a neighbor to the Tuans and sometimes eats breakfast at the inn. Watch him."

"Thanks for the warning, Pastor. I have been told he's getting more arrogant and threatening every day."

"John, Mr. Tuan came by the church yesterday and requested that I perform the wedding for you and Mai on the twentieth of April."

"The twentieth of April? Considering the war situation, that's a long time from now. I hope we're still here."

"I understand what you're saying. John, would you like to go with me Tuesday to a Montagnard village? I have a noon service in their church. The people in the villages need encouragement, especially during these difficult times. More than two hundred people usually attend the service."

"Yes, I would be happy to go with you. I've wanted to visit a Montagnard village and church. What time are you going?"

"We can leave Tuesday morning around ten. We'll go down the Saigon highway about ten kilometers and turn on a small road into the mountain area about five more kilometers."

"Pastor, I'll meet you at the Tuan farm. I'll leave my bicycle there. We'll be going on your motorcycle, right?"

"Right. I'll pick you up. See you then."

On Tuesday morning, Pastor Chanh met John at the Tuan farm, and they roared off toward the village. The small road off the main highway was rough and full of potholes.

When they arrived, Pastor Kar, the Montagnard pastor, and the church elders met them. Entering into the church building, John was surprised to see the sanctuary full with people standing in the back.

"There must be more than three hundred people here," John whispered to Pastor Chanh.

The people sang with fervor and enthusiasm. Pastor Kar introduced John as a special guest. Loud amens expressed the congregation's approval of his presence. Then Pastor Chanh began to bring the message.

The Montagnards spoke in the Koho language so Pastor Kar interpreted Pastor Chanh's words from Vietnamese into Koho. As he had done in the Sunday service, Pastor Chanh spoke with fervor and emotion. The congregation listened intently. Their faces expressed the deep emotion they felt upon hearing the Word of God.

Every day the Montagnard Christians lived in a life-or-death situation. They needed to be encouraged and challenged to live out their faith in the present crisis.

At the conclusion of the service, Pastor Kar asked John and Pastor Chanh to stay and eat with him and his family. "I did not plan on us staying," Pastor Chanh explained to John, "but it would be rude to turn down the invitation."

"No problem, Pastor. I'm glad to spend more time out here in the village."

The pastor's house was very simple with a sheet tin roof. The one large room that served as dining room and living room and the two smaller bedrooms had rough wood floors. The guests and Pastor Kar sat in the only chairs in the house.

"The family usually sits on a straw mat," Pastor Chanh explained to John. "When they eat, they place the food in the middle of the circle where they sit as a family. They eat with their hands except when they have guests."

John was hungry and enjoyed the steaming, hot rice and meat sauce served on top of it. The sweet hot tea refreshed him.

After lunch, Pastor Kar wanted to show his guests around the village. He spoke in Vietnamese to Pastor Chanh, who translated to John in English. He pointed out the rough fence that protected them at night from VC attacks. The five-feet-high barrier was made of logs and dirt with a deep ditch in front. Wooden spikes protruded over the edge to impale anyone trying to climb over.

The pastor spoke with pride about the local militia trained and ready to defend the village. "We have had a number of attacks," he told them proudly, "but we have repelled each one."

Pastor Chanh and John thanked Pastor Kar for his hospitality and the tour of the village. They knew they must get back to town before dark.

After he returned to the Tuan farm with Pastor Chanh, John told Mai all about his time in the village with Pastor Kar. He failed to notice the coming of dusk. When he finally dismissed himself, jumped on his bike, and headed for town, darkness closed in on him.

He traveled a kilometer down the highway when he heard someone calling from a clump of trees on the side of the highway. "John, John, here, here! Harry here. Stop! Come here!" John was startled, but there was no doubt it was Harry's voice.

"What do you want, Harry?"

"John, here. I tell you something. They kill you. You must come."

Getting off his bicycle, John pushed it toward the clump of trees. Harry was hiding behind a tree. "Minh and Viet Cong friends wait to kill you. Must not go down road. I wait for you."

"Where are they?"

"Not so far down road. Minh, two VC. They shoot you. You come; follow Harry."

John hid his bicycle under bushes and followed Harry. He led John on a trail that ran parallel one hundred meters from the highway. The tall trees and heavy underbrush shut out all light. John could not see anything. He followed Harry by sound rather than sight. Every half minute or so he reached out to touch Harry to make sure he was there. He was amazed that Harry could move so freely on the trail in the pitch-black darkness. It was as if he had night vision like a cat.

Suddenly Harry reached back and gripped his hand and led him off the trail. He whispered in his ear, "VC." As they crouched in the bushes beside the trail, John's heart pounded. At first he could not hear anything, but then he detected the muffled sound of footsteps. John could feel the presence of the Viet Cong as they passed within three meters of his hiding place in the bushes.

John and Harry waited several minutes until the sound of the Viet Cong footsteps faded down the trail.

"Now okay, John," Harry whispered.

Arriving at the inn, John felt a sense of relief. It was a home away from home for him, a refuge from the danger and hostility of the world about him. He shook Harry's hand. "Thank you, Harry."

Harry smiled briefly, but the smile was quickly replaced by a sober look. "Now dangerous. VC take Pleiku, Kontum. John go to Saigon. Bad here."

"I won't go to Saigon now, but I will be careful, Harry. Now I go to my room."

"Harry get you food, okay? You come."

Harry served John soup with French bread and cheese. After eating, John felt better. The tension began to ease from his body.

Going to his room, he lay on his bed and thought about the events of the day. He knew that once again he narrowly escaped death. He also knew if he remained in Lien he would face more attempts on his life from Minh and the Viet Cong. Yet he was determined to stay until he could marry Mai. He would not leave without her. He dozed off knowing that tomorrow would bring new dangers and new challenges.

13

Tuesday, March 18, 1975

With each day bringing more bad news about the collapse of South Vietnam, John examined his options once again. He talked with his friend at breakfast.

"Hal, if the Communist forces come into Dalat, will the Saigon highway still be open?"

"I think so. They are attacking toward the coast now. If they come this way they will come from Cam Ranh. This will give us time to escape down the Saigon highway. We can only hope that the VC won't block it."

"Will you loan me a taxi to get to Saigon?"

"Yes. You know I'll help you any way I can. I'll let you know when we must go. Don't worry."

"What about Air Vietnam?"

"Yes, you can try. We're just a few kilometers from the airport. You must check soon. They may be fully booked."

Shortly after the conversation with Hal, John rode his bike out to the Lien airport. Although it was still before eight o'clock, the terminal was packed with people. Some were on flights going out that day. Others were trying to book future flights.

John pushed and squeezed his way to the Air Vietnam counter. He caught the eye of one of the men behind the counter, hoping he spoke English.

"Are there any seats open to Saigon?"

The man had a harried look on his sweating face. "No, we're fully booked for the next month. Sorry. It's better for you to go by bus or taxi."

John pushed his way outside through the sea of fearful, desperate faces. He smelled the sweaty fear of the people pressing together.

On the way back to the inn, John passed the church and saw Pastor Chanh in the churchyard. He felt the need to talk to someone, so he turned his bike into the grounds.

"Pastor Chanh, do you have a minute?" he called. "I would like to talk to you about some things."

"Sure, John. Let's go to the house. Mrs. Chanh can serve us some of her fresh tea and cookies."

Mrs. Chanh greeted John with a smile. "John, we're praying for you and Mai. We know it is a difficult time."

John noted the contrast between Pastor and Mrs. Chanh and the people at the airport. The Chanhs were cheerful, relaxed, and helpful, while the people in the airport terminal looked as if they were on the verge of panic.

"Thank you, Mrs. Chanh. You and Pastor Chanh are an inspiration to me. I'm very grateful for the opportunity to become acquainted with you. I'll never forget you."

Drinking their tea, they discussed the latest war news.

"After they took Pleiku and Kontom," Pastor Chanh said, "the North Vietnamese are pushing on to the coast. The only South Vietnamese forces to stop them from going into Nha Trang and Cam Ranh are the Third Airborne Brigade straddling Highway 21 down the mountain from An Khe Pass."

"What will happen if they break through the pass?" John asked.

"Then there will be no one to stop them. I'll let you know what happens."

"Thanks, Pastor. I don't understand the language, so I appreciate you keeping me up on the news."

"One more thing, John, and again, it's not good news. My Montagnard friends tell me the VC are planning an attack on Lien. Our local forces know about it, but you need to be on the alert. Do you have a safe place to go when there's fighting in town?"

"Yes, Pastor. I have a good place."

On his way back to the inn, John stopped at a kiosk to buy toothpaste. A Vietnamese man approached him. "Hey, you American man, when you go I go with you, okay? VC will kill me. I worked with Americans. I want to go with you to America. You take me with you, okay?"

John sensed that he needed to say the right words to calm the man. "I am not going anywhere. I live here at the inn. I'm not going to America."

"You not go to America?"

"No. I'm staying here at Lien."

"America coming to save us, okay? Maybe they come tomorrow?"

John got on his bicycle. "Yes, maybe."

As John rode toward the inn, he felt sad. He knew America was not coming to save South Vietnam. He thought of Brad, redheaded Brad from his hometown, who was killed in a battle in 1972. Brad had fought to give the people of South Vietnam an opportunity to live in a free society. Thousands of other American GIs who died in Vietnam had believed they were fighting for a just cause. Now South Vietnam was going down the drain, and John felt a sense of frustration. He knew the complexity of the war, and he remembered the confusion he experienced during his tour of duty.

John thought about what Pastor Chanh had told him about the coming battle at An Ke Pass and how, if the North Vietnamese Army broke through, they would come storming down Highway One to Nha Trang and Cam Ranh. He must call the Burts and warn them. They might not know what was going on.

With that thought in mind, John rode his bike on to the post office. He called the Burts' house. No one answered. He thought of Ann and the children and feared for their safety at this critical time.

After lunch at the small cafe near the inn, John rode out to visit Mai and her family. He was concerned about the possible VC attack on Lien.

"Mai, Pastor Chanh said the VC might attack soon. Does your family have a safe place to go when there is an attack?"

"The Viet Cong never bother us. Until now we have never been attacked. My father does not talk about the war. He ignores the war. He sleeps all night and never asks or mentions anything about the fighting."

"Maybe the Viet Cong never bother you because Minh is your neighbor. They say he is a Viet Cong."

"Yes, I've heard that also. I don't know if that is true. His mother is a good neighbor. But John, you must be careful. You are the only American in Lien, and I'm sure the Viet Cong know about you."

"I'll be careful. Harry has a good hiding place. If the Viet Cong come, they'll not be able to find us."

John left the farm in the middle of the afternoon and went back to the inn. Harry was waiting for him.

"John, no go out of town again. Danger, John, danger. Maybe VC come tonight. We hide, okay?"

Tired from the tensions of the day, John went to bed early and slept soundly. When he woke, he looked at his watch. It was midnight, and the town was quiet. Maybe there would be no attack. He remembered Hal saying the Montagnards often warned the town about VC attacks that never came. He soon slept again.

The clatter of pots and pans from the kitchen told John Mrs. Dao and Harry were preparing breakfast.

Hal greeted him in the dining room. "Good morning, John. Did you sleep well?"

"Yes, I did. I thought the VC would attack last night, but I didn't stay awake waiting for them. You're here early, Hal. Do you have any news?"

"Yes, but it's not good. The South Vietnamese suffered a major defeat at Cheo Reo. Hundreds of our troops were ambushed and killed. Hue and Quang Ngai Province are under heavy attack by NVA forces. Thousands of refugees are pouring into Nha Trang. At least thirty thousand are in a tent camp on the edge of the city."

John thought about his missionary friends, Jeff and Ann Burt, and their two children and wondered how they were doing in this critical time. He would try to give them another call. After breakfast, he walked to the post office.

Ann answered the phone. "John, it's so good to hear from you! How are you doing? Are you preparing to leave Vietnam?"

" I proposed to Mai. She accepted and is willing to go to America with me. Please pray for us, Ann, for her family wants us to have a church wedding on the twentieth of April."

"The twentieth of April?"

"Yeah, and the way things are going, I don't think the country will hold together that long. I'm determined to leave Vietnam with Mai, but I don't know yet how everything will work out."

"John, we'll be thinking of you."

"How are you, Jeff, and the children doing? From what I hear, you'll need to leave Nha Trang as soon as possible."

"We're keeping in touch with Captain Thong. He's going to let us know when we need to leave. Please pray for us too. Hopefully we'll meet you sometime at some place. We want to get to know Mai. God bless you, John. I must go. There's a group from our church at the door."

Walking back to the inn, John felt a deep concern for the Burts. The war situation was deteriorating rapidly. What if they waited too long and failed to get out of the country?

14

March 22–23, Nha Trang

Saturday night, Jeff Burt was just putting the finishing touches on his Bible study. Someone banged on the front gate. It was Captain Thong.

"Pastor, I've just got a minute. My men need some rice. Can you give us two sacks?"

"Sure I can. I have two fifty-pound sacks."

"Thanks, Pastor. A battle is going on now below An Khe Pass. It doesn't look good for us. If the airborne troops can't hold, there is no one to stop the NVA from coming down Highway One to Nha Trang. If they break through, I'll send Brenda to tell you. You'll need to get your family out. And, Pastor, you need to go with them."

"Thanks. Is there any other way I can help you?"

"Well, yes, there is one more thing. When you get out, would you leave your car keys with Chi Ba, your house worker? If the NVA break through, I need all the transport I can get to evacuate my men."

"Yes, I will, Captain. May God be with you."

Captain Thong returned to his jeep where two of his men were waiting. They sped off into the night. The following morning as the Burts were about to leave for church, they heard someone pound on the front gate. Brenda stood there.

"Pastor, I don't have time to come in. Thong sent me to tell you the NVA broke through the pass. He said you should leave as soon as you can. I've got to go. Good-bye."

The Burts never saw Brenda again. They never knew what happened to her or Captain Thong.

Jeff stood for a moment trying to absorb the meaning of the fast-moving events. Then he wheeled and went back into the house. "Ann, that was Brenda at the gate. The NVA broke through the pass. Pack our suitcases. I'm going to the consulate to see about an evacuation flight."

The American Consulate seemed unusually quiet. After all, it was seven thirty on Sunday morning. Jeff asked the secretary if he could see the consul.

"Yes, he's in his office," she said. "You can go on in."

He knocked softly and entered. The consul sat at his desk staring straight ahead. His unshaven, red-eyed, disheveled appearance spoke of a sleepless night.

"Sir," Jeff said, "I was told by a Vietnamese friend in intelligence that the NVA have broken through An Khe Pass."

"Yes, that's correct." The Consul's faraway stare gave his face a dazed look. "The situation is critical."

"Sir, when can our wives and children be evacuated out to Saigon?"

"We'll get right on that tomorrow. Come by tomorrow morning. We'll be arranging flights out for American citizens on Air America."

When he returned home, Jeff saw that Ann had finished packing. "Ann, the earliest flights out will be sometime tomorrow. I'll have to check early in the morning. Let's go on to church. We need every opportunity to encourage our Vietnamese friends. They're going to be facing tough times."

"What about the other missionary families?" Ann asked.

"I'll tell them about the flight as soon as we get back. I'm sure they're all at church now."

The Burts were late for the worship service. Jeff could tell by the sober looks on the faces of the Vietnamese worshippers that they had heard the latest news. The pastor brought a message from the Forty-Sixth Psalm and exhorted the congregation to remember that their only real and sure refuge was the Lord God.

As the people filed out of the building Ba Chau, an older member of the congregation, spoke to Jeff. "Missionary, you should leave as soon as you can. Your presence here will not help us. You should leave Vietnam and go serve in another country. If you stay here, you will be put in prison or be killed."

Ba Chau's words shocked Jeff. He knew they were true. He would reevaluate how long he would remain in Nha Trang. Then it occurred to him that the time of his evacuation was in the hands of the consulate, not his own.

Jeff left Ann and the children at home while he drove on to the Good News Center. The center was already filled with refugees from churches in the northern provinces of South Vietnam. As he went about the day's activities there, the advancing forces weighed on his mind. How long would it take them to reach Nha Trang? Would there be enough time to get the wives and children out?

Promptly at eight o'clock the next morning, Jeff arrived at the American Consulate. This time he was not the only one. It was packed with American citizens. Many of them had Vietnamese wives and children. Everyone clamored to get a flight out. They knew the North Vietnamese Army was coming down Highway 1 and the time was short.

The secretary Jeff had met on Sunday morning called him to her desk. "You're a missionary, aren't you?"

"Yes. I have a wife and two children. There are ten other missionary families here in Nha Trang. Our wives and children need to be evacuated as soon as possible."

"I know. Let me introduce you to Mrs. Keegan. The Consul has placed her in charge of the evacuation."

The secretary led Jeff to Mrs. Keegan, a tall, personable woman with a soft smile. She was trying to communicate with a dozen people at one time.

"Mrs. Keegan, this is Jeff Burt," the secretary said. "He represents ten missionary families in Nha Trang. He wants to arrange flights for them to Saigon."

"Mr. Burt, we'll do everything we can to get your families out. However, the ambassador does not want us to panic the local population by quickly evacuating Americans. You can understand that, can't you?"

"No, I don't understand."

"Today we're going to start evacuating Vietnamese who worked for or still work with the American government," Mrs. Keegan continued patiently in spite of Jeff's response. "Come back each morning and check with me. Later this week we'll get your families out."

Jeff could not believe what he was hearing. He knew the danger increased with each passing hour. He felt his face flushing. "Mrs. Keegan, I know the situation is critical. My friend in intelligence has warned us to get out as soon as we can. We are American citizens, and you are responsible for our safety. At least evacuate our wives and children."

Mrs. Keegan leaned toward Jeff and put her hand on his arm. "Yes, Jeff, I understand. You come early tomorrow morning. I'll make arrangements for your wife and children. You men can go sometime later, okay?"

Jeff weaved his way out through the packed crowd. Would there be a "sometime later" for him and the other men?

15

March 25, 1975, Lien

At breakfast, Hal told John the imperial capital city of Hue had fallen to Communist forces and Danang was under heavy attack. Air America, Air Vietnam, and World Airways were evacuating hundreds of foreigners and Vietnamese from the Danang Airport.

"The Voice of America said Danang is in total chaos," he added.

Pastor Chanh dropped by after breakfast to talk with John. "I've only got a minute," he said. "You should not go out from town today, not even to the Tuans. I don't have time to tell you everything. Please, stay close to the inn."

The pastor sped off on his motorcycle headed south down the Saigon highway. John wondered if he planned on going to Pastor Kar's village. He worried for his safety. He knew the Viet Cong wanted to kill him.

All day John watched buses, trucks, and vans packed with people pass by going to Saigon. Somehow the fleeing throng thought Saigon would provide security for them. Ironically, to the North Vietnamese, Saigon was the main objective.

In the early afternoon, Harry told John the Communists were on the outskirts of Danang. The news of the battle for Danang swept over South Vietnam like a tsunami, intensifying the fear among the population. When a carload of fleeing travelers stopped at the cafe nearby, John saw the desperation on their faces.

John longed to see Mai, but Pastor Chanh's warning kept him from going out. Pastor Chanh was someone he trusted. The man knew something was happening. John would follow his advice.

The traffic on the thoroughfare was heavy. When vehicles stopped for refreshment, John wandered over to talk to those who spoke English. In every group of people he met, he could communicate with at least one or two. He asked them why they were going to Saigon and what they expected to do when they arrived.

"I want to leave Vietnam, but I have no plan for getting out," one man said.

Another man traveling with his wife told John, "We think Saigon is a safer place for us and it will be easier to find a way out if necessary."

Back to the inn, John asked Hal, "Hey, where are your taxis today? Are some of them taking passengers to Saigon?"

"Yes, I have two making the Saigon trip. Some are taking people to their home villages. One is taking some people to the coast where they hope to buy a boat and leave the country."

"What are your plans?"

"John, I would like to leave, but I have this fleet of taxis. People really need transportation now. Some of them are desperate to leave the area for one reason or another. Others fear what the Communists will do to them if and when they capture this area. Believe me, I'm not staying for the money."

"How about your family?"

"My wife wants to stay here. Her parents are old and will not leave. She says we're better off staying in our own house and community, but I think we should go to Saigon. Then we should try to go to America. My wife's older sister can take care of her parents. In America, we can start a new life and live in freedom from war and fear."

"I can understand how your wife feels, Hal. But you served in the military a number of years. If you stay, what will happen to you?"

"They would probably put me in prison for a while or send me to some work camp. I was just a sergeant major in the air force, not an important person; however, I probably could never get a good job. And my children would grow up under Communism."

"If you come to America, you'll be welcome in our home in Hopewell, Texas. I'll help you find a good job."

"Thank you, John. Some of the military people here believe the VC is ready to launch an attack on Lien. They are encouraged by victories north of us, but our local military is ready to fight. Stay alert."

"I will, Hal. Thanks."

John went to the cafe where he usually ordered fried rice. They were out of food. Dozens of travelers had eaten there from early morning until early evening.

He returned to the inn and saw Harry stirring about in the kitchen. "Harry, I went to eat at the café, but they have no food. Where can I eat? I'm starving."

"John, you no worry. Harry make you fried rice, okay?"

"Thanks, Harry."

After eating, John lingered in the dining room over a cup of coffee. He had noticed there were no guests at the inn the last few days. He asked, "Harry, why aren't there guests staying here this week?"

"John, we afraid. Maybe guests VC spies. We not take any guests now."

"That makes sense. In case of an attack on the town, you don't want VC in your inn. They say an attack is coming. Maybe tonight."

"Ya, maybe so. If VC come, we go to secret room, okay?"

Since he felt tired from the stress and uncertainty of the day, John went to sleep earlier than usual. He woke in the night and checked his watch. It was just after midnight. Maybe the enemy would not come tonight. They liked to attack when least expected.

With that thought in mind, John drifted off to sleep. He was jarred by an explosion and then another, and it was nearby. It sounded like a hand grenade. The *whump* of falling mortars from the national police station accompanied the chatter of automatic weapons all over town.

John quickly slipped on his clothes and shoes and then waited quietly on the edge of his bed. He heard the exchange of gunfire near the inn. The fighting was getting closer. He wondered where Harry was. As John was about to go look for Harry, he suddenly appeared with Mrs. Dao.

"John, much fighting. Not safe. We go to secret room, okay?"

John stood up to follow Harry. He quickly put his pillow under the bed cover to make it look like a person in bed; then he followed Harry and Mrs. Dao to the back room. Harry knelt, moved a throw rug, and lifted the door to the secret room.

Someone banged on the inn door. While Harry secured the secret door, a loud profane voice shouted and someone broke the inn door.

Crouching in the small room, John heard the pounding of his own heart and the short heavy breathing of Mrs. Dao. Two or three people moved around above them, banging and knocking over furniture. A short burst from an AK-47 startled their already jangled nerves.

Harry identified one of the voices. "Minh," he whispered.

When the banging and clattering of pots and pans stopped, they heard the VC leave the inn. After twenty minutes of quiet, Harry cautiously peeked out the secret door and looked around. "Okay now," he called down to John and Mrs. Dao. "VC gone."

John crawled out from the secret room and checked his bed and belongings. Just as he expected, the burst of automatic fire he heard went into his pillow. All of his belongings were intact except his bicycle. Someone kicked in the spokes on the front wheel.

"It was Minh," John told Harry.

Daylight was breaking as John worked with Harry and Mrs. Dao to clean up the mess of broken glass and other furnishings. With the exception of some broken windows and drinking glasses, not much damage was done. Evidently, Minh came looking for John.

While they were eating breakfast, Hal came in to report the results of the battle. "Our local militia put up a great fight," he said. "The VC outnumbered our forces, but our militia fought like tigers. They gave the VC a beating. Twelve VC were killed, and three of our local militia died. This is one battle they didn't win."

John felt concerned about Mai and her family. He also wondered about Pastor Chanh. He borrowed Harry's bike and went to the farm. Mai ran out to meet him.

"John, you're all right? We heard the shooting and explosions in Lien, and we prayed all of you would be safe."

"We're all okay. It was an all-out attack, but our forces beat them."

"Did they attack the inn?"

"Yeah, VC broke down the door and came into the inn. They did some damage but not much. They were looking for me, but Harry, Mrs. Dao, and I hid in our secret place. They didn't find us. We think Minh was leading them."

"Are you sure?" Mai asked.

"Yes, we're sure. Harry recognized his voice."

"I'm very sorry for Minh and his mother."

"Have you heard anything from Pastor Chanh? Yesterday he went to Pastor Kar's village. I felt uneasy about him going outside town."

"Pastor Chanh came by our house on his way back from the village. He only visited a few minutes, but he said his visit went well. Four men from the village militia rode with him to our house. They didn't come in but turned and went back right away."

"How did Pastor Chanh's family make it through the attack last night?"

"A church member came by this morning and told us the pastor and family had fighting near their house, but they are safe."

"I'm happy to hear that. Pastor Chanh and his wife are a source of encouragement for all of us."

After getting on Harry's bike, John paused. "Mai, the war is closing in on us, and I don't think we'll make it to April the twentieth. You know I'm not leaving without you, don't you?"

"We must keep on praying and trusting God, John. He'll make a way."

"Your faith—it encourages me. I'll try to pray more and stop worrying. I want to do something. I don't know what to do. I feel like…like a spectator watching a giant wave move toward me that will sweep me away."

"Last Sunday Pastor Chanh spoke about our faith being tested during this war time. I think our faith is being tested, John."

"Yeah, I think you're right. We need to be faithful. Sometimes I want to run and take the easy way out, but I need more patience. Mai, being here with you, Pastor Chanh, and the other Christians has taught me a lot about patience and waiting on the Lord."

John's faith would be tested even more in the days ahead.

16

When John arrived back at the inn, Harry proudly presented him with his repaired bike.

"Now John can go on bike."

"Thanks, Harry. You're a great help to me."

" Minh kick John's bicycle. Maybe have sick foot."

"I hope so. Maybe he cannot walk to cause more trouble."

But John knew that was wishful thinking. Minh and his VC friends would be walking about and causing more trouble. He knew it, and most of the people in Lien knew it also.

Minh grew up on a farm neighboring the Tuan's farm. He was the youngest of three children. His older brother and sister worked for an export company in Saigon. Unlike Minh, who only finished middle school, they completed high school and two years at a business college.

When his older siblings came home to celebrate Tet, the Lunar New Year, Minh felt uncomfortable around them. He sensed their superior attitude. "*Em* (child)," they ordered, "bring us some tea and sweets." Minh resented being treated like a servant and seethed with anger for weeks after his siblings returned to Saigon.

Minh was ten years old when his father was assassinated. The murder affected Minh's childhood. An already shy and reserved child, he became more of a loner. He dropped out of middle school to help his mother with her vegetable gardens.

When he was seventeen, he met Tham, who worked on a neighboring farm. Tham, two years older than Minh, was a member of the local Viet Cong Party. He liked Minh and began to influence him to join. Minh showed only casual interest at first, but he became more inspired as the war heated up.

The main reason for Minh's fascination with Viet Cong was his hatred for America. He believed the rumor that Americans were behind the assassination of his father. After his twentieth birthday, Minh joined the Viet Cong.

Minh attended school from first grade to middle school with Mai. Although he never spoke to her about how he felt, his "puppy love" for her never diminished. In a moment of candidness, he shared with Tham that he wanted to marry Mai. Tham, a blabber mouth, told other members of the party.

Minh met with the Viet Cong cadre and eight other VC in a wooded area two kilometers south of Minh's house. The attack on Lien had not gone as planned. Minh noted that three of his comrades were missing from the meeting. They were among those killed in the attack.

The cadre, a stocky man in his middle thirties, worked for a prosperous farmer seven miles north of Lien. Minh's father had worked with the same man.

"We've got to keep pressure on the local militia until our comrades from the North get here," the cadre said. "Every day they're getting closer to total victory. Soon our party will be in control of this province. When that happens, each one of us who have been faithful party members will share in the fruits of victory."

"Comrade," Tham asked, "when can we come out in the open and tell everyone who we really are?"

"Not now. Be patient. The time is near when we can march downtown and take over the leadership of this area."

"There is an American living in Lien," Minh said. "He was a soldier, and he has come back to stir up the local population. He needs to be taken out, and I can do it."

The cadre laughed. "Minh, we all know why you want to kill the American. He is planning to marry the girl you like."

The group joined the cadre in a moment of laughter at Minh's expense. Minh's face flushed, and an angry scowl creased his brow. "He's our enemy, and he should be killed. He has no business in Vietnam."

"Yes, you are right." The cadre saw Minh's anger and tried to moderate his feelings. "He is our enemy. But wait for the right time. When we come into power, all of our enemies, including this American, will be dealt with in an appropriate way."

Tham asked, "What are we going to be doing while we wait for the North Vietnamese? We should settle scores with our enemies, like the Montagnards. They have made life miserable for us."

The stocky cadre stood to his feet. "We'll meet again Wednesday evening, same place, same time. Then we'll discuss our future actions in the countryside."

With those instructions, the cadre disappeared into the dark woods. The other VC members left, each in his own direction. Minh and Tham left together, walking toward Minh's house.

Minh still felt angry about the cadre poking fun at him. "I think our cadre is lazy. He does not live in this area, and he does not know what's going on. He wants to lay back and do nothing until the NVA comes."

"Yes, I agree with you. We should be striking at those who have taken action against us. Why wait for the North Vietnamese? I do not trust them. They think they are better than us southerners."

"Tham, you stay with me. We will kill the American, and we will choose our time to do it. After that, we will choose someone else to take out."

"You can count on me. I'll stay with you."

When Minh and Tham approached Minh's house, they saw the faint glow of the lamp through the pulled curtains. "Mother is still up. She always waits for me to come home."

"Your mother does not care for me," Tham said.

"You know how mothers are. They want perfect friends for their children. After she gets to know you, she will like you."

"You know, I never had a mother. My aunt raised me. I was nothing more than a servant for her family. When I was fifteen, I ran away and started working for Mr. Bao. He works me hard, but he treats me right."

"I know your father was killed during President Diem's time, just like my father. I think the Americans were behind it. Their spies worked with the Montagnards and other traitors."

Tham said, "I was only a boy when my father was killed. I remember very little about him. My mother said he was a strong Buddhist. One day he led a protest march in Saigon, and President Diem's soldiers shot him."

"Tham, we have a lot in common. You don't want to walk home alone. Do you want to sleep at my house tonight?"

"No, I will go home. I'm used to walking in the woods at night. I will see you next week. If you need me, let me know."

Minh softly pushed open the front door. His mother was sitting by the lamp, reading. "Mother, you are up late. You should be in bed, not waiting up for me."

"Son, I worry about you when you are out late. I have no idea who you are with or what you are doing this time of night."

Minh patted his mother's hand. "I was just out talking with Tham and a few other friends. We have a good time telling stories. You should not worry about me."

"You know you are all I have now. Your father is gone, and your brother and sister are in Saigon. I seldom ever see them. You are the only one."

Minh saw the mist in her eyes. He reached out and squeezed her arm. "Mother, I am always here for you."

"Child, let's go to bed. I'm going to get up early and take my vegetables to the market with the Tuans."

"Ya, I need to be up earlier than usual to drive my truck to pick up a load of gravel for the airport. Mr. Hao wants me at the inn at five thirty."

If Minh's mother had known about his nighttime activities, she would not have slept at all.

17

March 25, Nha Trang

Jeff and Ann Burt enjoyed living and serving in Nha Trang. They both spoke fluent Vietnamese and knew the culture of the country. Although there were tense times, they didn't feel their lives were in danger. They went about working with the churches and serving the people in their community.

Their elementary-aged children attended a school sponsored by one of the church groups in the city. The Burts had many friends in both the Vietnamese and expatriate communities. But their happy, fruitful time in Nha Trang was coming to an abrupt end.

Mrs. Keegan at the Consulate booked the missionary wives and children on an Air America flight to Saigon.

"The flight is at ten fifteen," Jeff reminded Ann. "We can't be late."

Ann was putting the last of their mementoes in the suitcase. "What else do I need to carry? I've got our wedding photos, pictures of the children, slides of the work here, and a few special gifts given to us. Can you think of anything else?"

"Nah, just be sure you have your best clothes. Pack carefully since you're allowed just one suitcase. I'll be allowed one when I come, so I can bring some of your clothes and other things later.

"Yes, I've left what I want you to take on the bed. Jeff, would you please bring my sewing machine when you come?"

"Sewing machine?"

"Yeah, my portable sewing machine. You know how we shopped around to find it, and I really like it. You can hand carry it, can't you?"

"Yeah, I'll bring it. Don't worry."

Just before leaving for the airport, Ann walked through the house. She enjoyed making this house a home. Her decorative talents were evident in the beautifully arranged house. Each piece of furniture and picture was in the right place. They enjoyed so many happy times in their home and entertained so many guests.

Ann touched her favorite vase and ran her fingers over it, lingering for a few moments. Standing before her favorite painting, she tried to absorb every detail. Somehow she knew she would never see her house again.

"Ann, we must go now," Jeff said. He knew it would not be easy for her. When she turned toward him, he saw tears in her eyes. He hugged her for a moment.

As they were getting into their car, Jeff was pleased to see Josh and Marie excited about their trip. They didn't realize the significance of the moment.

Jeff said, "Josh and Marie are happy about seeing their friends in Saigon. They don't realize they will probably never be back to their home here. It's just as well. Some things are too heavy for children to bear."

When they arrived at the airport, they saw that the other missionary families were already there. The children playing in the small terminal called out happy greetings to Josh and Marie. The husbands stood quietly beside their wives.

Both husbands and wives realized the significance of their parting. The country was rapidly falling to the invading Communist forces. Anything could happen. Already, there was a breakdown of law and order in Nha Trang. The situation was deteriorating hour by hour all over South Vietnam.

At the boarding call, the husbands gave their wives and children tender and loving hugs and then watched the DC-3 aircraft taxi out and roar down the runway. Each turned away lost in his own thoughts and whispered prayers. Would there be time for them to be evacuated to Saigon?

When Jeff Burt returned to his house, he felt a surge of sadness and loneliness. He already missed Ann and the children. He knew he had to keep on the move. There were people to encourage, refugees to feed, and programs to set in place. He could be evacuated at any time. He would have only one opportunity to leave on an Air America flight. He needed to work with his leadership to set plans for the future.

Jeff was a self-starter. He grew up on a farm where hard work was the norm. Upon graduation from high school, he joined the marines and did a tour of duty. After discharge, he felt called to the ministry. Along with financial help from the GI Bill, he had to work to meet his financial needs in college. In the summer, he worked full time selling Bibles door to door.

Looking back on that experience, Jeff laughed. Selling Bibles prepared him for anything else he wanted to do in life. It was tougher than the Marines. Now he needed to call upon that training, experience, and discipline to meet the demands of the times.

When he arrived at the Good News Center, Jeff saw more than sixty refugees eating their noon meal of rice, vegetables, and shrimp. He was pleased to see local church members cooking and helping minister to the needs of those that had fled their homes before the invading NVA forces. After lunch, they would have a devotional time, and in the evening, there would be a worship service.

One of the church leaders and two young people approached Jeff. "Missionary, can you go with us to the refugee camp? We want to distribute eight bags of rice and Gospels of John."

"Yes, I can go. Where are the bags of rice? We can load them into my van."

While the rice was being loaded, six more young people squeezed in. Jeff was glad. They could use the extra help. "How many refugees are in the tent camp?" Jeff asked one of the young volunteers.

"Thirty thousand plus. They are still coming in from north of here."

Before arriving at the camp, the Vietnamese leader mapped out a plan of action. "I'll take six of the teenagers and distribute the rice to heads of the families," he explained to Jeff. "Each must show his family papers and the number of family members. In this way, we'll make sure the rice is distributed equally among the people."

"I'll take two people with me to give out copies of the Gospel of John to those who want them," Jeff added. "If someone wants counseling, we'll try to help them."

The ministry team was overwhelmed with the needs of the refugees. A man came running up to Jeff. With a choking voice, he said, "We left Pleiku in this caravan with hundreds of people. My wife and two children were separated from me. I can't find them. I don't know where they are. Can you help me? Can you pray for me?"

Wherever they went, people asked for help finding a missing wife, child, or husband. The hurt, grief, mental pain, and trauma were greater than the physical needs.

When the ministry team had finished the rice distribution, the Vietnamese leader asked, "Jeff, are you going to attend the evening service at the center?"

"I don't know. I'm exhausted—in every way—and can't think straight now. I've never experienced anything like this. So many ... so many families separated, so much sorrow and grief. It's too much."

On the way back to Nha Trang, few words were spoken. Each person had been impacted by the enormity and tragedy of war. Jeff dropped the ministry team at the Good News Center and drove the two blocks to his house. He ate a snack and lay down to recoup his strength so he could attend the evening service with the refugees.

The spirit of the service was electrifying. Most of the worshippers experienced the trauma of losing loved ones or barely escaping with their lives. Many stood to give testimonies of praise and thanksgiving to the Lord Jesus Christ for His mercies and grace. When the sermon was given, the congregation leaned forward in eager attentiveness to catch every word. They were living life or death situations, and they wanted to hear the Word of Life. They knew they were facing the fires of persecution or even death.

Praying in his heart, Jeff committed himself to the Lord Jesus to be a more useful servant and witness for the Master. Life was so fragile and uncertain. He committed himself to making the rest of his life count for eternity.

Jeff felt uneasy walking home in the dark. Soldiers who had deserted their units prowled the city with M-16 rifles. He walked quickly to his house, locked the gate, and slipped into the front door. The house was dark and quiet.

The tension and trauma of the day caught up with him, and he felt drained. He missed his family. To the chatter of automatic weapons in the distance, he crawled into bed wondering what the night and the days ahead held for him. He slept fitfully as did people all over the city of Nha Trang.

18

March 26, Nha Trang

Captain Thong was a patriot. He was sickened about the turn of events. He knew South Vietnam had the ammunition, weapons, and soldiers to repel the North Vietnamese invasion. He could hardly believe how quickly the provinces were falling before the NVA onslaught.

He was appalled at the tactical mistake made by President Thieu to abandon the highland cities and command the divisions there to retreat to Nha Trang.

He told Lieutenant Tra, "Our President should have known better. They were dug in at Pleiku and Kontum and had enough ammunition and artillery to make a fight out of it. They could have tied up the NVA for months. With that time, we could have gotten international opinion and material support on our side."

"Yes, and maybe the Americans would have sent their bombers again," Lieutenant Tra said. "But sadly, the retreating divisions have been cut down and rioted by the NVA. Any military man knows how vulnerable retreating forces become. The few soldiers who reached Nha Trang are deserters from General Phu's division."

"With the defeat of the Third Airborne at Highway Twenty-one, we have no choice but to abandon Nha Trang. But we're not abandoning the fight. We're going to run so we can fight again. Lieutenant, you know the military term for that, don't you?"

"Yes, sir, Captain—guerrilla warfare."

"Correct. And you know that if the enemy captures us, as officers in intelligence, they're going to torture us to try to get all the information they can and then shoot us."

"Yes, sir. Our options are limited. We can never surrender, so we'll fight. When the main forces move on toward Saigon, we can harass them from behind. Guerilla warfare can slow down and even tie down enemy forces for some time."

"That's what we're going to do, Lieutenant. We have one hundred and twenty men in our unit. We only want volunteers to fight with us. The others can go home to their wives and children."

"Captain, we might be able to recruit other soldiers from other units to join us."

"Yes, some of these soldiers roaming around Nha Trang deserted because their officers deserted them. Let's check with as many as we can. Some of them may want to fight with us. You work on that, Lieutenant, and I'm going to destroy all of our intelligence documents."

Captain Thong depended on Lieutenant Tra to see that his orders were carried out. Lieutenant Tra had been assigned to work with him since his graduation from the National Military Academy in Dalat, the West Point of South Vietnam.

Tra was born and grew up in Danang. The youngest of seven children, his father was a province chief during the Diem Regime, and his mother taught in a Catholic school. Tra was intelligent and studious. His mother wanted him to become a teacher, but from his early childhood, he was fascinated with the military.

Standing five feet ten inches tall, Tra carried himself with an erect military posture. He seldom smiled and often had a melancholy, faraway look as if he saw something no one else could see. Yet he was exact in military matters. His light complexion and thin nose revealed his grandfather's French ancestry. Tra was handsome, and more than once it was said he looked like Charles Boyer, the French movie star.

Captain Thong also had another important mission. He sent his driver to get Brenda at their house. She was to be on the early afternoon Air America flight to Saigon. The following day she would leave Saigon on a Pan Am flight to the States.

He thought of the previous night. He had tried to assure her: "Brenda, you don't worry. You go to San Antonio and rent us a house. I'll come later. I've got to stay with my men as long as possible. I'll feel better if you're out of the country and safe." But even as he tried to assure her, he knew in his heart he would not be coming later. He was committed to his country, and that commitment probably meant death.

After picking up Brenda, the driver came for Captain Thong to accompany her to the airport. When she was ready to board the flight, Captain Thong embraced her. He was not an emotional person, but in that moment, his feelings welled up so that he could hardly speak. "I love you, Brenda."

"I'll see you soon in San Antonio, Thong," Brenda said with affected cheerfulness. "Please take care of yourself."

Captain Thong stood on the tarmac until the DC-3 cleared the runway and roared off toward Saigon. He doubted that he would see his wife again. But Captain Thong was a soldier, and he was on mission.

He hurried back to his office to meet with his officers. He sent one of them with five soldiers to get a truck and put as many barrels of gasoline on it as possible. They needed at least three more trucks for troop transport and three to four more jeeps.

Each of the officers was assigned to a specific task. One was to get as many bags of rice as he could on a truck together with other food supplies. A junior lieutenant was assigned to be the ordnance officer. Captain Thong ordered him to secure a truck and get ammunition, hand grenades, and mines together with mortar tubes and shells. They were to move out for the mountains the following day.

Rather than meet in such a conspicuous place as Captain Thong's office on Beach Boulevard, they assembled five miles outside Nha Trang in a grove of coconut trees off the Saigon highway. Eighty-five volunteers met Captain Thong and his three officers. Seventy of the men were from the intelligence unit, and fifteen were recruited from among the deserters.

They formed a convoy and headed toward Cam Ranh on Highway 1. At Cam Ranh, they turned right onto a smaller highway and headed up the mountains. After forty kilometers, they connected with Highway 11 from Phan Rang toward Dalat.

"We're going to a village forty kilometers from Dalat located at the foot of the mountains," Captain Thong informed his men. "It's the village of Song Nghia, home of Sergeant Huy."

"Captain, my village will be honored to welcome us who have chosen to continue fighting for our country," Sergeant Huy said.

"The villagers will support us," Thong continued, "because most of them have family members killed by the Viet Cong. We'll set up camp two kilometers from the village on Sergeant Huy's uncle's farm, and we'll be moving from time to time."

Eighteen kilometers up Highway 11, Sergeant Huy signaled from the lead jeep that the convoy was to pull off on a dirt road to the right. The vehicles moved slowly on the narrow dirt road that led to the village of Song Nghia.

Two kilometers farther the convoy pulled into the village to a warm reception. Thong and Huy had sped ahead to prepare for the soldiers' arrival. The village chief and villagers welcomed the contingent of soldiers as heroes.

"We, the patriots of the village of Song Nghia, want to welcome you faithful soldiers of the Army of the Republic of South Vietnam," the chief announced. "You are our heroes. Later on this evening, the women will prepare a feast to honor you."

The warm welcome met an important need for Captain Thong and his unit. They needed to be recognized and respected for who they were: patriots and heroes. This warm reception encouraged and strengthened them for the fierce battles that lay before them.

19

March 26, Lien

Sometimes a man wants to be alone, to get away from the herd, to break away from the main stream of society, and exercise his right to run free. John woke feeling a need to get away, to go some-where to think.

"Don't go outside of town alone," Hal warned a number of times. "It can be dangerous. You are watched by the Viet Cong."

John knew the VC started their activities around three o'clock in the afternoon, so, in spite of the warnings, he decided he would get an early start and return before noon.

After eating breakfast, he left on his bike as usual toward the Tuan farm. But this time he didn't stop there, he continued down the Saigon highway. Early morning sun lit the mountainside and found drops of dew on leaves, weeds, and grass and turned them into sparkling diamonds.

John breathed in the fresh, crisp mountain air and pedaled faster. He felt a sense of exhilaration at being alone and free. After an hour of pedaling, John worked up a sweat. He could feel the drops rolling down his nose and taste the salt on his lips.

After twelve kilometers, he pulled off to rest. A truck heading toward Lien came barreling down the highway. When it passed, John recognized Minh as the driver. And Minh recognized him. The truck stopped and backed into a small side road.

Aware of Minh's intentions of coming back for him, John pedaled quickly to a small road leading to a farmhouse three hundred meters ahead. He heard the roar of Minh's truck and the screeching of brakes on the highway behind him. John hoped Minh wouldn't turn off the highway, but he heard the truck coming with a low, steady roar.

John raced toward the farmhouse. Maybe they would help. He pounded on the door, but no one answered. The truck labored down the trail, not yet in sight but close. He pushed his bike behind the barn and hid it in a clump of bushes. A few seconds before the truck came into view, he ran into a cluster of trees beside the barn. He hid behind the largest tree and peeped out to see what Minh would do.

Minh stopped the truck in the farmhouse yard, jumped out, and pulled his AK-47 rifle from behind his seat. He glanced around and then pounded on the farmhouse door. When no one answered, he tried to force the door. The thick door did not bulge, so he went to the back of the house and looked around. Then he went to check the barn. He went inside, and John could imagine him looking into every stall and space. He heard boots climbing the ladder to the loft and the rifle poking around in the hay.

John weighed his options. While Minh was in the barn, he could run back to the main highway. But what would he do then? His bike was hidden in the bushes. But Minh would continue to search for him, and eventually he would look in the cluster of trees. John realized the danger of his location, so he left his hiding place and sprinted toward the highway, keeping out of sight in the trees.

Minh began to search the trees around the farmhouse. Not finding his prey, he started his truck and drove back toward the main road.

From his hiding place near the highway, John heard the truck coming and congratulated himself on outsmarting Minh. After the truck passed, John walked back to the farmhouse and got his bicycle. He felt good about escaping his enemy and pedaled back toward the main highway.

Just when he came around a bend in the road, he saw Minh some hundred meters away coming toward him carrying his rifle. John had underestimated his enemy. Minh had driven half a kilometer down the highway toward Lien, parked the truck, and walked back toward the side road, rifle in hand.

Minh was as startled as John. He lifted his rifle to fire, but John whirled the bike around and pumped with all his might toward the farmhouse. By the time Minh came around the bend, John was out of sight.

John hid his bike in the same clump of bushes behind the barn and then darted among the trees toward the highway again. If the plan worked once, maybe it would work again.

By the time Minh arrived at the farmhouse, John had passed the halfway point back to the highway. When he reached it, he saw a truck traveling toward Lien. He waved and thumbed at the truck but to no avail.

He had to keep moving. He broke into a trot toward Lien. Minh would be back in his truck and on the highway in a short time. John had to flag a ride quickly or get off the highway. He saw a car coming. He waved his thumb, but the car never slowed down. Then two more cars passed.

When he came around a curve on the highway, he saw a truck parked on the side of the tarmac. It must be Minh's truck. Looking inside the cab he saw, to his surprise, that Minh, in his haste, left the keys in the ignition.

John did not hesitate. He climbed into the cab, started the truck, and roared off toward Lien. He laughed out loud visualizing Minh's face when he came back for his truck and found it missing. He would know John took it. He let out a cowboy yell—e-e-e-yo—and shouted, "Walk home, buster! Walk home!"

When John pulled up in front of the inn, he saw one of Hal's taxis. He needed to meet Hal, tell him what had happened, and give him the key to the truck.

"John, what are you doing driving one of my trucks?" Hal asked at the door.

"Am I glad to see you!" John replied. "You'll never believe what happened. Minh saw me on my bike about twelve kilometers down the Saigon highway. He came at me with his rifle, but I escaped into the woods. When he came looking for me, I doubled back to the highway. I tried to flag down some cars, but nobody stopped."

"But how'd you get the truck?"

"When I ran down the highway, I came upon the truck. I couldn't believe the key was in the ignition. So I hopped in and took off."

"Glad you got the truck, John. I knew Minh was a VC, but I gave him this last day to work. Minh will never work for me again."

"Here's the key."

"Would you drive it to my house? I'll follow you and bring you back."

20

Friday, March 28, Lien

It was one of those clear, crisp, sun-filled days that character-
ized the time of year before the rainy season in the highlands. John
enjoyed the morning as he rode his bike to the farm. He slept well
and felt refreshed. At that moment, the war seemed so far away.
Birds were singing, people worked in their fields, and children were
going to school. No one would ever guess there was a war going on.

When he arrived at the barn to park his bike, John saw Mai running out of the house to greet him. She squeezed his hand. "Hello,
John. It's a beautiful day. After we finish our work, let's go on a
picnic."

"Great idea. Just you and me?"

"Yeah, just you and me. We won't go far. There's a trail that will
take us to a nice grove of trees. We can eat under the trees, okay,
John?"

"Okay. That sounds great!"

While they were talking, Mr. and Mrs. Tuan came out of the
house and greeted John. They went into the barn briefly and then
returned to the house.

"My mama and papa are not feeling well today," Mai explained, "and my younger brothers and sisters went to school."

She made a good-natured grimace. "You and I are the only workers today."

"Mai, I could work all day with you and never get tired. You are so beautiful. I am inspired and invigorated whenever I look at you."

Mai blushed. "Come on, John. Let's go."

Mr. Tuan wanted them to work with the cabbage and spinach. They went about their task laughing, talking, and enjoying one another's presence. They forgot about the war, the world, and everything except each other.

At noon, Mai went into the house and got the picnic basket she had prepared. John took it from her.

"Is it safe out in the forest?

"Ya, we'll only go about two hundred meters. I often take my brothers and sisters there to play or to have a picnic. Don't worry. No VC in the daytime."

Usually no Viet Cong prowled around that time of day, but Mai and John did not know that danger lurked in the woods near the Tuan house. Minh was without a truck and a job. He knew John came often to the Tuan farm, so he waited nearby. Upon hearing voices and laughter, he hid among the trees. Taking the trail, John and Mai walked in the luxuriant forest.

"Look, there are wild orchids," John exclaimed.

Different kinds of flowers grew beside the trail. Mai pointed out wild fruit trees growing among the tall trunks. "Some of this fruit is good to eat and some is not," she said.

"How do you know which you can eat?" John asked.

Mai laughed. "You have to learn them. My papa taught me when I was a small girl. I know all about the outdoors, the plants, fruits, and animals."

"Is there wild game here?"

"Fifty or more years ago, Dalat was the game-hunting capital of Vietnam. The French organized hunting parties going out from Dalat."

"What did they hunt?"

"Deer, wild boars, tigers, even elephants."

"Elephants? You mean there were elephants in this area?"

"Yes, there were many elephants in Vietnam. Only a few are left because of the war. There are still some deer and wild boars, but they stay deep in the forest." Mai stopped. "Here's our special place."

The picnic spot was to the right of the trail. A babbling brook ran through a grove of tall, dense trees that closed out the sunlight so there was little undergrowth.

Mai took a cloth out of the basket and spread it on the ground. Then she brought out boiled eggs, French bread, jam, fruits, and *cha gios*. She knew John liked *cha gios,* Vietnamese rolls. They sat on the side of the long cloth and ate, talked, and laughed.

Minh watched from his hiding place. His anger seethed at them laughing and talking together. He thought about running back to his house to get his rifle, but he ruled that out because of Mai. He had known her all of his life. Since he was eight years of age, he had dreamed of marrying her. No, he would not endanger her life by shooting John when they were together.

John told Mai about the house he was planning on renting from his aunt in Hopewell, Texas. "It has three bedrooms, two baths, a large living room with adjoining dining room, and a nice-sized kitchen with a dishwasher."

"A dishwasher? What is a dishwasher?"

John smiled as he thought about how much fun it would be showing Mai new technologies in America.

"A dishwasher is a machine that will wash plates, cups, glasses, eating utensils, bowls, even pots and pans. You put washing powder in it and turn it on. Hot water comes pouring in to wash the dishes cleaner than we can wash them."

"John, you can teach me how to use the dishwasher and other things."

"Yes, I'll teach you." John smiled. "I'll show you how to use all the appliances."

"Appliances? What are appliances?"

"Well, an appliance is a machine made to do something special. Like the dishwasher is made to wash dishes. We have a machine—an appliance—made to open cans, one to cook food, and one to keep the food fresh. We have many appliances."

"I'm excited about going to America. You will teach me about how to use all these … these … appliances, won't you?"

"Sure. I'll teach the most beautiful and most intelligent girl I've ever known to use everything in the house. And I'll teach you how to drive a car."

"Drive a car? Will we have our own car?"

"Yes, we'll have our own car, and you will learn to drive it."

"John, I'm worried that your family will not receive me. I'll be different from them."

"You don't worry about that, Mai. My family will love and receive you as a daughter. My sister will absolutely adore you, and my brother will be fascinated with you."

"Your church?"

"My church will be thrilled to have you as a member. We're one of the friendliest churches in Hopewell. Our pastor is a godly man who loves Jesus and preaches God's Word. You'll like our church."

"John, sometimes I become afraid when I think about going to America, but I love you, and I want to go with you."

John took Mai's hand and drew her to himself. "I love you, beautiful girl. You never need to be afraid, okay?"

"Okay. John, did you have a special girlfriend in America before you met me?"

"No, I did not have a special girlfriend in America. You are the only special girlfriend in my life."

John leaned toward Mai and kissed her again and again.

"I love you, Texas cowboy," Mai responded with a dimpled smile.

The way Mai in her Vietnamese English emphasized "Texas cowboy" sent John into convulsions of mirth. "Texas cowboy? Where did you get that?" he said between bursts of laughter.

"John, we must go home now," Mai said with a sudden serious expression. "My brothers and sisters are home from school. Mama and Papa will want me to show them their afternoon work."

They gathered the cloth and leftover food and walked, talked, and laughed all the way back to the house.

Mai and John never knew that Minh spied on their special picnic. It did not spoil that peaceful and perfect day. But it was the calm before the storm. Angry and frustrated, Minh watched them walk back to the house. He decided what he would do, and with that thought in mind, he raced through the woods to his house.

Minh kept his rifle hidden in the barn and wrapped in a burlap bag. John would ride his bicycle back to the inn, so Minh would run back to the highway and ambush him. When Minh reached the barn, his mother greeted him.

"Minh, since you have been laid off from your truck driving job, you can help me with the garden and other things that need to be done. The eggs can be gathered, and the chickens need to be fed."

"Ya, I will, Mother. Just tell me what needs to be done."

"Why have you been running? You are sweating and breathing like a dog chasing a deer in the woods."

"I am going to meet a friend, Mother, so I hurried back here to get something."

"You young people are always in a hurry. Your friend Tham came by to see you. I don't care for him. You need to be careful who you make friends with."

"Tham is a good friend, Mother. He can be trusted."

"Just be careful." She turned toward the house. "Bad friends can get you into bad trouble."

When his mother had gone, Minh went into the barn, lifted a board from the floor, and took out his rifle. He unwrapped it, put in a cartridge magazine, and slipped out the back of the barn into the woods.

He broke into a run. He would wait beside the highway about a kilometer from the Tuans. The American would not escape this time. Minh would empty the magazine at him. Minh raced through the woods, dodging trees. Sweat poured down his face and darkened his shirt. He heard the sound of a bus laboring up an incline. That meant he was near the highway. Another minute and he would be there.

Minh burst out from the woods to the edge of the tarmac. When he glanced down the highway, he saw John just disappearing in the dusk, pedaling toward Lien. Minh felt disappointed and disgusted, but he knew there would be another time. The American would not leave Vietnam alive. Most certainly, he would not leave with Mai. Seething with anger, Minh walked back through the woods toward his house.

21

Friday, March 28, Nha Trang

John Gunter had enjoyed a peaceful day in the highlands, but Jeff Burt felt the tension and uncertainty of a breakdown of law and order. The police and army units abandoned the city to lawless criminals and whoever wanted to take control by force.

Driving toward the consulate, he saw an increased number of ARVN soldiers on the streets, most carrying M-16s. He heard the news that the Third Brigade Airborne suffered defeat in the battle near Ninh Hoa at Highway 21. The increased number of soldiers in the city must have been those who escaped the battle.

Jeff, along with everyone else in Nha Trang, realized the North Vietnamese Army would come storming down Highway 1 to Nha Trang any time now. He saw that the city was shut down. Stores were locked and boarded up to keep out looters. There were daily reports of robbing, raping, and looting by ARVN deserters.

Hundreds of people were gathered in front of the American Consulate building. Most were Vietnamese, but some were Americans. Jeff was thankful that he cultivated a relationship with the consulate personnel, including the Marine guards. He called earlier and talked to Mrs. Keegan, who was handling the evacuation flights out to Saigon.

"Get on down here as early as you can," she exhorted him. "This may be the last day we can get you out."

After Ann and the children had left for Saigon, Jeff had become so involved in working with the refugees he put off going to the consulate to arrange his flight. One afternoon he drove by but was discouraged to see a huge crowd waiting outside. Another day he was told to check later in the week.

Now it had come down to a must-go situation. He did not want it to happen this way. The consul did not urge Americans to get out. On the contrary, Americans were being evacuated very slowly to avoid panic among the population.

Earlier in the week, Jeff talked with one of the consulate administrators whom he knew from the English language worship services. He asked him, "Why is the evacuation process coming along so slowly?"

"The ambassador still thinks South Vietnam can be saved," the administrator said, "and he's slowed down the evacuation process for the consulates. Now it's come to a crunch, and we don't even have a plan. We're just shooting from the hip trying to get everybody out that we can. You'd better get a flight out now."

With that exhortation, Jeff went to the consulate early Thursday morning, and Mrs. Keegan arranged this Friday morning flight out for him.

"We have just received word that Danang is about to fall to the North Vietnamese Army," Mrs. Keegan told him. Jeff sensed her fear and desperation along with all the consulate personnel and the crowd of people waiting for flights to Saigon.

Before leaving the house, Jeff left his second set of car keys with Chi Ba, the house worker, and instructed her to tell Captain Thong the car would be at the consulate parking lot. He did not know Captain Thong left for the mountains two days ago.

A fifteen-foot green fence surrounded the embassy with a large gate to allow vehicles to come and go. A smaller gate led to the front office. Jeff parked half a block from the embassy since the crowd prevented him from driving through the large gate.

The vocal, impatient mob of Americans and Vietnamese pressed together, pushing and shoving one another. With difficulty, John squeezed through to the small gate.

"I need to see Mrs. Keegan!" John shouted over the crowd to the marine standing guard behind iron bars of the locked inner gate. "I have a flight."

The guard moved closer to the gate and cupped his hand to his ear.

"Mrs. Keegan, Mrs. Keegan!" John shouted. "I need to see Mrs. Keegan to get my flight voucher!"

The marine guard hesitated a moment and then stuck his head into the embassy door and called for Mrs. Keegan. She appeared and saw Jeff.

"Mr. Burt, I'm sorry, but you will have to go out tomorrow!" she shouted with her hands cupped around her mouth. "We have to get out the Vietnamese dependents today. Come tomorrow at eight."

Jeff wanted to say something to Mrs. Keegan, but she disappeared into the building. Tomorrow? There might not be a tomorrow. Why was he, an American at his country's own embassy, put on hold?

Jeff drove back to the house. Just as he got out of his car to open the gate, two South Vietnamese soldiers carrying M-16s walked by.

"Let's rob this American," one of the men said, not realizing Jeff understood Vietnamese. "What's he doing here anyway?"

Jeff knew he must not show any fear. He looked the soldiers in the eye. "I am a missionary. You soldiers should not go around robbing people. If you're not going to fight the enemy, go back to your own villages."

The surprised soldiers looked sheepish. "We're sorry, Pastor. We didn't know you were a pastor. Excuse us."

As the two soldiers walked on, a teen worker from the Good News Center who had seen what was happening said to Jeff, "Pastor, you must be careful. There's a breakdown of law and order. One of us needs to be with you when you go outside your house."

"Thanks," Jeff replied. "I'll be at the center the rest of the day."

Jeff spent the remainder of the day working with the church team at the Good News Center, ministering to the needs of the sixty refugees being housed there.

He dreaded the coming night and what it might bring. Many rumors were floating around. "The North Vietnamese Army is poised to charge into Nha Trang early tomorrow morning," someone said. After the evening worship service, two men escorted Jeff to his house.

Jeff slept fitfully through the night. The continuous chatter of gunfire echoed through the tense city nervously waiting for the uncertain events of the coming day.

Waking at the crack of dawn, Jeff wondered if there would be another flight out of Nha Trang. Would he even make it to the consulate?

22

Saturday March 29, Lien

Pastor Chanh arrived at the inn as day was breaking. He had never come that early before, so those who saw him knew he must be on a mission. The two early birds, John and Hal, already sat in the dining room.

"Hello, Pastor Chanh. You're out early this morning. Is there a problem?"

"Yes, I'm taking medicine out to Pastor Kar's village. His wife is very sick. One of the men came to the parsonage late yesterday and brought me Pastor Kar's request."

"What is she sick of?" John asked.

"The pastor thinks she has pneumonia. Last night I hurried to the pharmacy and got penicillin and aspirin as he requested. Now I'm taking them out to the village."

"Pastor, you must be careful," Hal said. "The VC are moving around stronger than ever before."

John agreed. "I wish some of the Montagnards would go back and forth with you."

"This is the reason I'm going early. The VC prowl all night and sleep until noon. I plan on going straight to the village, deliver the medicine, and be back before the VC start moving about."

Pastor Chanh quickly drank his coffee and sped off on his motorcycle. The fresh morning air felt crisp, clean, and cold. He was glad he thought to wear his leather coat instead of his cloth jacket.

He knew Mrs. Kar must be very sick for the pastor to request medicine. She really needed it last night, but she must have it this morning. Pastor Chanh felt good about being able to help his fellow believers. They risked their lives to keep him safe several times. Delivering this medicine was a small way of showing his gratitude.

When he arrived at the village, several men met him and promptly escorted him to Pastor Kar's house. They knocked on the door, opened it, and went into the front room. The pastor, looking very drawn and tired, came from the back bedroom.

"Thank you for coming, Pastor. Thank you. My wife is so sick. She is breathing very hard now."

"I brought penicillin. She needs to be given this right away. She must take two of these tablets every four hours. You must make sure she takes all of them. If she begins to feel better, do not stop giving her the tablets.

"Do I give her water with the tablets?"

"Yes, give her a full glass of water. Now here is another kind of tablet. This will help to break up the congestion in her lungs. Give her one in the morning and one in the evening also with a glass of water."

"Thank you," Pastor Kar said and disappeared into the bedroom.

After several minutes, Pastor Kar emerged again. "Would you please come and pray for my wife?"

"Yes, I will," Pastor Chanh said. He followed his fellow pastor into the bedroom. He placed his hand on the hot forehead of

Mrs. Kar and prayed for her healing and full recovery. He ended his prayer by praying, "Father, heal her for the sake of Your name and for the sake of Your pastor and Your people. In Jesus's name. Amen."

They returned to the front room and were served hot tea and rice cakes. For several minutes, they discussed the critical situation in the country. Then Pastor Chanh stood.

"Excuse me, I must return to Lien while it is early morning. You know that the later it gets, the more dangerous it becomes."

"That is true. You need to go quickly. Some of my men would go with you, but many of them are out working, and others are patrolling the area."

"I will be all right. It is still early, and I will ride fast."

Pastor Chanh started his motorcycle, waved at his friends, and went down the road to the Saigon highway. A kilometer from the main highway, he saw a log across the dirt road. He knew immediately it was an ambush. He hit the brakes and slid to a stop while turning the motorcycle around and heading back in the direction he had just come from. Gunning the motor, he heard the bark of an AK-47 and several bullets whined by him.

He gained speed and thought for a moment he might escape. But fifty meters in front of him in the middle of the road stood six VC with automatic weapons.

With bullets whizzing around him, he whipped off the road and went into the woods, dodging trees. Seeing a dry creek bed off to his right, he slid the motorcycle between two trees to get on the bed. He roared down the creek bed some thirty meters before the creek evolved into a trail. The trail ran parallel with the road.

Pastor Chanh gunned his motorcycle hoping to put distance between himself and his pursuers. But he hit a pothole, and it threw the cycle out of control. His body went one way, and the motorcycle went the other. Unhurt, he jumped up, ran to his motorcycle, and pulled it upright. He heard the VC coming down the trail. The motorcycle must start. He stomped down on the paddle. It caught with a roar. Once again he sped down the trail with bullets clipping the trees around him.

If only he could make it back to the village, he would be safe. He couldn't outrun the VC, but he stood a chance if only the trail would go near enough to the village. If he could get within half a kilometer, he would meet Montagnard guards.

The trail widened. Pastor Chanh sped up so his pursuers were more than a hundred meters behind. *I might,* he thought once again, *escape from my enemies.* Just then the trail ran out. It stopped on the edge of a ravine. No motorcycle could cross it.

He leaped off the cycle and sprinted into the woods. But he would be no match for the Viet Cong on foot. They closed in on him from two directions.

Pastor Chanh ran until he was completely exhausted. He could run no more. For the sake of his family and his church members, he did everything he could to save himself, but he was not afraid to die. If God permitted him to die, he would die trusting the Father.

He knelt behind a tree. He could hear the VC closing in on him. It would not be long now. He prayed for his wife and children and lifted up his church people. He asked the Lord to give them courage and strength to meet the testing and challenge of the days ahead. Then he prayed for his enemies. "Father, in some way penetrate their hearts with Your love. Forgive them, Father, and have mercy on them. Father, I commit myself into Your hands."

The early morning quiet was shattered by a burst from an AK-47.

When Pastor Chanh had not returned by noon, Mrs. Chanh sent her younger brother to the inn to ask if anyone knew his whereabouts.

"We have not seen him since he left for the village early this morning," Harry told him.

The fact that Pastor Chanh had not returned home became a source of deep concern for all who knew and loved him. John was worried for he knew Pastor Chanh's commitment to help others had led him on a dangerous mission.

In the middle of the afternoon, a Montongnard Christian came to the inn from Pastor Kar's village. John could hear him speaking in a low, terse voice. Since they were speaking in Vietnamese, he could not understand them. He watched the expressions on the faces of Harry and Mrs. Dao and knew the news was not good.

After the Montagnard Christian had left, Harry turned to explain the news to John. There were tears in his eyes. He could hardly speak. "Pastor Chanh, he die. VC kill him. Now he dead."

John went to his room and lay on his bed. He was shattered and confused. How could the Lord let such a great man of faith die like that? Everyone needed his positive faith and his presence. He was such an encouragement to others.

Then John remembered what Pastor Chanh had said to him weeks before. "I'm not afraid to die. If I die, I go to be with Jesus."

Suddenly John felt ashamed for questioning the Lord about Pastor Chanh's death. Pastor Chanh belonged to the Lord, and he could not die until the Lord permitted it. Now he was in the presence of Jesus. The real Pastor Chanh would live forever. A surge of faith and hope strengthened him.

Pastor Chanh's death prepared John Gunter for the time of fiery testing coming upon him in a short while.

23

March 29, Nha Trang

Before seven, Jeff drove to the consulate. Mrs. Keegan said come early, so he came early, remembering the large crowd the day before who blocked him from going into the consulate parking lot. He hoped someone was there to open the gate.

He knew on regular days the consulate didn't open until eight. But this was not a regular day. As a matter of fact, this might be the last day. A crowd had already gathered in front of the smaller gate. At the large gate, he stopped and blew his horn. A Vietnamese worker peered through the peephole of the gate and then swung it open. Jeff drove in and parked his car.

The consulate personnel were scurrying about like a flustered flock of chickens. Some were shredding papers; others seemed uncertain as to what they should be doing.

In the office, he found Mrs. Keegan. "Jeff, I'm glad you're here early. You'll be on the first flight out at eight forty-five. The bus will leave at eight twenty. It's only a ten-minute drive to the airport."

At eight twenty, Jeff boarded a packed bus taking people to the airport to catch the Air America flight out to Saigon. It revved its engine until the Marine guards opened the large green gates to the consulate parking yard. As soon as the gate swung open the bus roared out, barely missing a dozen or more people desperately trying to stop it.

Jeff looked back. The crowd was even larger than the previous day. Everyone appeared frantic, pushing, shoving, and yelling.

When the bus turned right on Beach Boulevard, a group of ARVN soldiers pointing M-16s tried to commandeer it, yelling for it to stop. But it roared on toward the airport. It passed the terminal crowded with hundreds of people desperate to escape Nha Trang and parked beside the waiting Air America DC-3 with its engines ready to go.

The bus driver yelled for everyone to get onto the plane as fast as possible. After the last passengers had boarded, a crowd of fifty or more people came charging toward the aircraft in an attempt to force themselves onto the flight. The DC-3 roared off down the runway, barely missing several of them.

Jeff Burt didn't realize it at the time, but he was on the last bus from the consulate. The situation had become so dangerous that buses could no longer be used to evacuate people. The remaining evacuees and the consulate personnel were taken out by helicopter.

When he arrived in Saigon, Jeff was met at the airport by fellow missionary Jack Landers from their mission office. Surprisingly, the phone system had been still working when he left his house that morning. He had called the mission office and requested that someone meet him at the airport.

Boarding a waiting van, Jeff voiced the tension that built up within him. "Jack, this country is falling apart. There's chaos in Nha Trang. We've got to get our wives and children out of this country while we can."

As Jeff ranted, Jack calmly listened. Driving through downtown Saigon, Jeff saw that people on the streets were going about life as usual. A large crowd gathered in front of a movie theater. Jeff couldn't believe what he was seeing. He came from the chaos and confusion of a city that collapsed and was on the verge of being taken over by enemy forces.

Then he realized what was happening. Saigon was cordoned off by some of the best troops in South Vietnam. The chaos and confusion of defeat, fleeing refugees, and the breakdown of law and order had not yet reached Saigon. No wonder Jack was looking at him so strangely. He didn't understand what Jeff had come from. He couldn't, no one could, unless they had been there themselves.

Jack's response brought him back. "Jeff, your family is staying at our house. Would you like to go there now?"

"Yes, I would."

Jeff had a joyful reunion with Ann and the children. He spent the next two hours answering many questions about the people and activities in the city. He told about the last frantic days and how glad he was that Ann and the children were not there.

Still thinking of the last few hours in Nha Trang, Jeff said, "Ann, I want us to book a flight out of Saigon as soon as possible. The country is falling apart."

"Is it that bad? The missionaries here don't seem alarmed. They know things are bad, but no one has left yet. Most of them are going about life as usual."

"Yes, I've noticed that, and I can't believe it."

"After you've had a good night's sleep, you can put everything back into proper perspective. Our ambassador still thinks the Vietnamese troops can hold a line thirty miles north of Saigon and save this southern part of Vietnam. He believes if the ARVN can hold for a while, the international community will do something to save the South."

"Really?" Jeff looked at Ann.

"Jack and Joy have invited us to eat out with them tonight at the American Club and afterward see a movie. *Paper Moon* is playing with Ryan O'Neal. Would you like to go? A change of pace would be good for you. You've been under a lot of stress."

Jeff really didn't want to go, but he sensed that Ann wanted to get out for the evening. "Sure," he agreed, "we'll go."

The American Club was unbelievably luxurious. Small chandeliers hung over beautiful black mahogany tables set on thick, rich red carpet. On the stage a band played and a Vietnamese woman in an evening dress warbled out a song in a deep, throaty voice. A Vietnamese waiter in a white jacket and bow tie took their order. Everyone ordered steak.

Ann carried on most of the conversation for the Burts.

"Jeff, you're not saying much tonight," Joy Landers remarked. "I'll bet you're tired, aren't you?"

"Yeah, a little tired. Maybe the steak will pick me up."

Actually Jeff was almost in a state of shock. He was in a city that was carrying on as if there were no war. He sat in a rich club about to eat steak with his wife and friends, listening to a band and a singer. A few short hours earlier he was in a deteriorating situation where people were desperate to get out of the way of danger. It was almost more than his emotions could bear. He had a slight headache.

His mind drifted from the hum of table conversation to Nha Trang. What were the church people and refugees doing? He would rather have been there worshipping with them tonight. This was all so superficial, like fiddling while Rome burned. No one realized the days of this club were about to end.

The next day Jeff booked a flight to Singapore for his family. "I don't want us leaving on the last flight out," he told Ann. While making arrangements, Jeff thought of their friends. "Ann, I wonder what happened to Captain Thong and Brenda. I never heard from them after the night he came by for the bags of rice. And what about John Gunter? As I remember, he said he planned on taking forty days to find his sweetheart, marry her, and take her out of the country. We know he found her, but the forty days are about up. I wonder if he will make it out."

Jeff and Ann Burt left Saigon for Singapore not knowing what happened in the lives of their friends. If they knew, they would have spent more time praying for them.

24

Mountains Near Dalat

Late in the evening, Captain Thong gathered his band of guer-rillas for a briefing. The last two days squads of guerillas had been eliminating Viet Cong units operating nearby. The VC units had no inkling that South Vietnamese guerilla forces were in the area.

The guerrillas had just eaten. They sat in a semicircle around their leader. Looking over his troops, Captain Thong felt a sense of pride.

"These are the real patriots of Vietnam," he told Lieutenant Tra. "They know we will all probably die in battle, but they're ready and unafraid."

Captain Thong took a deep breath and laid aside his wave of emotion. He had to prepare these men for battle in the coming days.

"Men, I've just received word that Cam Ranh has fallen to the advancing NVA Tenth Division. The Tenth will be coming up this highway, maybe even tomorrow or surely the day after tomorrow, to take Dalat and Tuyen Duc Province. Our scouts will bring word about their movement. We want to hit and harass them along the way."

Captain Thong paused and knelt down on one knee. "We want to be like waiting and wounded tigers. You know, our ancestors often hunted tigers in these very forests. If they wounded a tiger, the animal would hide and wait to pounce on his pursuers. We are wounded tigers. We'll wait, ready to pounce on the enemy when he comes up the mountain."

After the opening exhortation, Captain Thong and his lieutenants briefed the men on the plan of action for the coming ambush. "Tomorrow morning a truck will take twenty land mines five kilometers down the mountain to the steepest and most crooked curve," Captain Thong explained. "They will be stashed among the nearby trees and bushes ready to be placed and armed at the appropriate time."

"Will someone guard the mines?" Lieutenant Dang asked.

"Yes, the demolition team will stay with them. When they receive word that the Tenth Division is coming, they will set ten mines in and alongside the highway. After the first trucks detonate the mines, a squad of guerillas will open fire on the NVA convoy."

"What's the plan for engaging them in a firefight?" Lieutenant Tra asked. "They're an entire division."

"Yeah, I know. When they return fire, one of our squads will feign a swift retreat into the woods. The NVA will pursue them. Our main body will be waiting in ambush three hundred meters down the trail. The other ten mines will be planted along the trail where the ambush is to take place."

"Sounds like a good plan, Captain," Lieutenant Tra said.

Before daybreak the next morning, trucks loaded up. Captain Thong cautioned the men moving the mines. "Take care to conceal your movements. The NVA have eyes and ears all over South Vietnam. Every farmer along the highway could be a Communist spy."

The guerrillas waited all day for news from their scouts, but no word came. Captain Thong was concerned. His mind whirled.

"What if they have captured our scouts?" Tra asked. "They will be tortured and may disclose the ambush plan. Then we'll be the ambush victims. Why haven't we heard from our scouts?" At that moment, a guerrilla came running up. He reported that one of the scouts had just arrived from down the mountain. In a few minutes, he was brought to Captain Thong.

"Captain, I'm sorry I am so late in coming to report. I know you were waiting to hear from us. We were busy gathering information up until late this afternoon."

"What happened with our forces in Cam Ranh?" Captain Thong asked.

"The Tenth had a hot battle with the ARVN, but the North Vietnamese overcame them with superior firepower and numbers. The fighting was so fierce the Tenth needed a day to refurbish their troops. Our troops fought them to a standstill but were finally beaten down."

"When is the Tenth moving up this way?"

"My projection from all the information we've gathered is tomorrow."

"Where are the other scouts?"

"They're in position near Cam Ranh, Captain. As soon as they know of any troop movement, they'll get word to me. I'll be waiting at the halfway point for any word. When I hear from them, I'll speed up to you."

"Good work, soldier," Captain Thong said. "You scouts are to be commended for a job well done. You're the eyes and ears of our strike force. We are depending upon you. May God go with you."

After the scout had eaten and refreshed himself, he sped off on his motorcycle to position himself. The guerrillas found a good spot to spend the long night on the forest floor and then unrolled their blankets. Long after the last soldier was asleep, Captain Thong, his back against a tree, remained alert. In his mind, he was going over all the contingencies in the coming ambush. After midnight, he finally fell asleep. He would need his rest to meet the demands and dangers of the coming day.

25

March 31, Lien

While Captain Thong's guerrillas set up their ambush, a sad procession drove slowly into Lien. Hal in one of his taxis brought Pastor Chanh's body back to his church. A group of twenty Montagnard Christians accompanied Hal on their motorcycles. Members waited to wash and dress his body before placing it in a coffin. Mrs. Chanh and the family members came to spend time with him.

From four until eight o'clock in the evening, church members and the public viewed the pastor and paid their respects to his family. Hundreds of mourners came from Lien, Dalat, and the countryside. Crowds of people filled the church. Leaders decided to extend the visitation hours to accommodate the large number of people.

John went to the church with Mai and her family. He could see from Mai's red eyes that she had been crying. He tried to comfort her. "Mai, Pastor Chanh is in heaven now. We'll miss him very much, but he's with Jesus."

"Yes, I know, but it is so sad that he was taken from his wife and children. He was such a great pastor and friend," Mai whispered with a catch in her voice.

Hal took the Tuans home in his taxi. When he returned to the inn, John was waiting for him.

"Hal, what time is the funeral tomorrow?"

"Ten o'clock. The pastor from the largest Protestant church in Dalat will be conducting the service assisted by Pastor Kar and another pastor from Dalat."

"How is Pastor Kar's wife?" John asked.

"She is doing better. A man from their village told me she ate some soup, her first food in days, and drank two glasses of hot tea."

"I'm so glad," John said, "for Pastor Kar and his wife are great servants of the Lord, and the people need their spiritual leadership. Hal, why did the Viet Cong kill Pastor Chanh? He was such a good man who loved everyone and wanted to help anyone in need."

"The pastor advocated a free South Vietnam. He stood for everything the Communists are against. He helped the Montagnards, so the Communists thought he worked with the CIA and South Vietnamese intelligence."

"Pastor Chanh was not political. We know that he only wanted to minister to people in need."

"Ya, John, you're right. But the Viet Cong have overplayed their hand. The rumor is the Viet Cong and North Vietnamese leadership are not pleased with the murder of Pastor Chanh. They want the general population to look upon them as liberators, not murderers."

The church was packed long before the ten o'clock hour set for the funeral. Several hundred people stood in the churchyard. The war was put aside as the local population came to pay respects to a humble servant of God and spiritual leader.

Pastors and church leaders arrived from Dalat in dark suits and took seats on the platform. Pastor Kar arrived on a motorcycle.

Government leaders of Lien came accompanied by military leaders in dress uniforms.

Hal and John accompanied the Tuan family. On the way into the church, John noticed local militia stationed around the building and along the roads leading into town. John took a seat with the Tuans near the front of the auditorium.

The Protestant church choir opened the service with two of Pastor Chanh's favorite songs. Pastor Kar and the pastor from Dalat read Scripture and brought words of tribute to the fallen martyr.

"We are not only here to grieve the death of a beloved husband, father, friend, and fellow servant of Jesus Christ," Pastor Kar began his message. "We are also here to celebrate his life lived so wonderfully for the glory of our Lord."

After the funeral and burial, John walked back to the inn deep in thought. He felt a great emptiness that he had lost a friend who understood him so well. Harry met him and pressed his hand as he went into the inn. Harry seemed to sense his need.

"John, sit down. Harry get you tea and sweets, okay?"

"Thanks, Harry. I am happy I know you. Now I know more than ever before how important it is to have good friends."

Harry smiled and nodded, but John was not sure he understood what he was trying to say. John was so grateful Harry sensed how he felt and wanted to encourage and help him.

While John drank his tea, Hal came into the room.

"Hal, come and have a cup of tea and some sweets with me," John said. "I need to talk with you."

"Thanks, John. I can use something to drink and eat."

"Tell me what's going on with the war. I haven't heard anything since Pastor Chanh's death."

"I hate to bring bad news at this time, but it is not good. The North Vietnamese have defeated a South Vietnamese unit in a fierce battle at Cam Ranh. They will be coming up this way. There's nothing to stop them now. The local militia will just melt into the population, and you can't blame them. They're no match for the NVA."

"You mean they could be invading Dalat and Lien in a few more days?"

"That's right, John. This is a good time for us to talk about a plan to get to Saigon. I want to get my family there so we can get a flight out to America. I don't want my children living under a Communist government. I like America, and I think my family will like it also."

"I think they will enjoy living in America. You can live near us, Hal, and we will help you adjust to living in the States. I can help you get work. You already speak English well, so you can get a good job."

"Thanks. I would have left for Saigon sooner, but many people here need my taxi service. As soon as I hear that the NVA is moving up the mountain, I will tell you. I can loan you one of my taxis so you can take Mai and her family with you to Saigon."

"Do you think Mr. Tuan and his family will go? Do you think Mr. Tuan will allow Mai to go if they choose to stay?"

"I don't know, but we need to talk to them now. Time is very limited. When we have to leave, we will have to go quickly. We need to know for sure who will go with you. Let's go now."

In the taxi, John's pulse quickened. The situation was out of his control, but he knew he had to act while he had time. What if Mr. and Mrs. Tuan would not give their consent for Mai to go with him? He had to have a plan B. John was still turning over the possibilities in his mind when they arrived at the Tuan house.

26

Friday, April 4, Mountains Near Dalat

The North Vietnamese Army's Tenth Division swept down Highway 1 to bypass Nha Trang, for their intelligence confirmed that the South Vietnamese had abandoned the city. The NVA charged on down Highway 1 to Cam Ranh to engage the waiting South Vietnamese troops. After the South Vietnamese Forces put up fierce resistance, they over-powered them.

At the break of dawn, the Tenth began moving up the mountain toward Dalat. When the guerrilla scouts were sure of the Tenth's direction, one of them sped on his motorcycle to the halfway point. He made contact with a fellow scout at a kiosk owned by a one-armed ARVN veteran. The scout jumped on his motorcycle and raced to give word to Captain Thong and his waiting guerrillas.

The scout raced round a curve and turned into a small trail in a dense forest. He was quickly escorted to Captain Thong.

"Captain, the Tenth began to move at daybreak. They should be here in the middle of the afternoon. They're moving slowly with their artillery and other baggage."

"How far ahead of the main convoy is the recon team?" questioned Captain Thong.

"About a kilometer."

"And how many men are on the team?"

"Between twelve and fifteen."

Captain Thong turned and spoke to his lieutenants. "We'll let the recon team go on up the mountain. After they pass, the demo team can quickly get the mines out on the highway. We don't want the recon team setting off the mines meant for the trucks."

It was the middle of the afternoon when they spotted the recon team in a captured ARVN jeep and a Japanese-made truck approaching the curve. As the scout reported, they were about a kilometer ahead of the main convoy. They passed by, unaware of the waiting guerrillas watching them. When they rounded the next curve and were out of sight, the demo team set and armed the mines and then covered them with ragged burlap sacks as if some local farmer threw them away.

In fifteen minutes, the guerrillas could hear truck motors laboring up the steep incline. The nose of the lead truck poked around the curve closely followed by others. The guerrillas squatted in the bushes beside the highway waiting for the trucks to detonate the mines.

The lead truck missed the first mine, but the second truck hit it. The explosion lifted it several feet in the air, sending twenty soldiers flying in different directions. They landed like limp rag dolls. A split second after the first explosion, the lead truck hit the second mine and suffered a similar fate.

The following trucks stopped. Troops piled out of the next one with weapons ready. The guerrilla squad swung into action, pouring automatic fire into the startled soldiers. Most of them were killed or wounded under the intense fire of the guerrilla squad.

The Communist troops in the other trucks began to fire on the guerrillas. As planned, they retreated, backing into the forest. A platoon was ordered to go in after them. The retreating guerrillas fired from cover as they moved from tree to tree. The troops were at a distinct disadvantage as they entered the dense forest.

Two men went down under a burst of fire when they advanced only ten meters into the forest. The platoon poured automatic weapons fire into the trees toward the sound of the guerrillas' fire, but with doubtful results.

The NVA commanders wanted the guerrillas eliminated or at least driven far back into the mountains. They could be dealt with later. But they didn't want to leave them near the highway to harass their troop movement. Thus they sent a platoon after the fleeing guerrillas.

When the platoon advanced thirty yards into the forest, they were ambushed by Captain Thong's waiting guerrillas. The platoon suffered heavy casualties.

The commander of the Tenth Division, General Than, shook his head as he received reports about the ambush. "They did what General Giap taught us to do—open fire on the enemy and lead them into an ambush. Their leader is a good military man. We'll have trouble with this group."

A different kind of struggle was going on in Lien.

27

John and Hal arrived at the Tuan house. The family came out to greet them. They must have realized the significance of their coming. As for John, he was glad Hal had come with him. In the delicate communications with Mr. and Mrs. Tuan, he would need someone besides Mai to interpret.

The parents took them to the guest room and served hot tea. After a few minutes of polite talk initiated by Hal, John began to inform the Tuans about the war situation.

"The North Vietnamese have taken Cam Ranh, and they will be coming to invade Dalat and this province either tomorrow or the day after," John said.

John waited as Hal translated what he said. He could tell Hal was adding extra explanations.

"Hal is taking his family to Saigon in one of his taxis," John explained carefully. "He has agreed to loan me a taxi. I would like to take you, Mai, Mrs. Tuan, and your family to Saigon with me. Once we get to Saigon, it will be safer for us."

After Hal interpreted, Mr. and Mrs. Tuan talked between themselves for several minutes. Then they spoke to Mai and Hal for several more minutes. Although John could not understand their words, he could see Hal's gestures and animation and knew he was trying to communicate the gravity of the situation and the options involved in staying or going. When their conversation was finished, Hal spoke to John.

"Mr. and Mrs. Tuan do not want to go to Saigon. They will stay here with their younger children. But they are willing for Mai to go with you to Saigon. I told them you would try to go on to America, and they said Mai could go with you to start a new life in your country."

John was moved by their willingness to let Mai go. He knew Pastor Chanh's death had turned their world upside down. Before the loss of Pastor Chanh, they were not willing to let Mai go without a church wedding. Only when death came so close they realized the seriousness of South Vietnam's situation.

With Hal continuing to translate, John said, "Thank you for entrusting your daughter to me. You know that I love her, and my family will love her. I promise to take care of her and provide for her needs. While we are in Saigon, I will try to get a Protestant pastor to marry us."

"We believe you love her and will provide for her," Mr. Tuan replied.

"I am sorry we could not have the wedding here with you and our friends," John continued. "However, God in his providence has not allowed us time for a wedding. But we are confident God will provide what we need, and we will continue to trust in Him."

Mai and her parents seemed pleased with John's expression of gratitude. Mr. and Mrs. Tuan nodded their heads in affirmation and patted their daughter.

"When are you leaving?" Mr. Tuan asked.

"I can come to get Mai and her suitcase late tomorrow afternoon," Hal said. "She can stay at the inn with Dao. My family and

I will also stay at the inn until our departure. We will leave about four o'clock in theafternoon."

On the way back to the inn, both John and Hal were quiet with their thoughts. Hal broke the silence. "John, you know our plan, but anything can happen. We need to be ready to move out at any time."

"I'll be ready, Hal. They say Saigon is cordoned off some fifty kilometers around. Once we get inside that cordon, we'll be safe."

"We'll go down Highway Twenty to Di Linh and on to Bao Loc," Hal explained. "Once we get to Bao Loc, we'll be okay."

"When we get to Saigon, I'll confirm my ticket and buy one for Mai. You can buy tickets for your family on the same flight."

"How about passports, John? Will my family all need passports?"

"Yeah, they each need passports from the South Vietnamese Government and visas from the American Embassy."

"Can we find someone to help us with the visas?"

"As soon as we reach Saigon, I'll call my missionary friends, Jeff and Ann Burt. They'll know someone to help. I want to find a preacher or missionary to marry Mai and myself. It will be easier for me to get her out of Vietnam as my wife. I'll call my family and have them meet us at the airport in Dallas. You and your family can go with us to Hopewell, okay?"

"Thank you, John. I am happy about going back to Texas. I will become a cowboy, yes?" Hal's smile lightened the tense moment.

"We'll get you cowboy boots and a cowboy hat, Hal. You'll be a Texas Vietnamese cowboy." John laughed.

They were both grateful for a few moments of levity. They knew stressful times lay ahead.

Since Minh was without a job, he spent more time with the local Viet Cong and his friend Tham. Minh's mother did not like Tham, so they would meet in the barn or the nearby woods.

Minh passed Tham some important news. "This morning the American and Hal visited the Tuans. I don't know all the details, but I think they will try to leave by taxi to go to Saigon.

The information did not surprise Tham. "Are you sure?"

"No, but when Hal is involved, you know they're planning on using his taxis."

Tham, from his squatting position, poked the ground in front of him with a stick. "Let's get our garage boys to watch the inn and find out what's going on. You may be right. The American could be planning on leaving soon."

"The garage boys live near the inn. I'll contact them right away."

"Will Mai go with the American?" Tham asked.

Minh blushed. "I think so. We've got to make sure he doesn't go anywhere."

"Yeah." A faint smile creased Tham's face. "We'll stop him before he leaves town."

"But we have got to be careful and not hurt anyone besides the American," Minh said with great concern.

"We will watch for the right opportunity. Do not worry. No one else will be shot."

"Do not forget," Minh said, "we meet with our unit this evening. Our cadre has something important to tell us."

"Our cadre always has something important to tell us. He does not know what's going on in our area, but he wants to tell us what and how to carry out our mission here."

Minh said, "I'm going now to get our helpers to check out things at the inn."

28

When Hal moved two taxis to the front of the inn, Minh's friends reported it to him.

The two were teens who worked in a garage, orphans adopted and reared by the owner for labor. They were nothing more than slaves to do his bidding. He fed them well and gave them small amounts of money for entertainment on Sundays. But he beat them when they were stubborn or failed to do what he expected. They had been kicked around all their young lives. So when Minh paid attention to them, they were open to him.

Minh had been talking to them for a year, convincing them he thought they were important. He asked them if they wanted to be in a party that would soon be in power. They were interested and were soon drawn into doing things for the local Viet Cong. They looked up to Minh, which made him feel important also.

The Viet Cong met in the forest near Minh's house. The cadre, who had grown up in Dalat, squatted along with the others. Most of his life he worked on vegetable and fruit farms. But there was no doubt about who was leader. He exuded quiet strength and a commanding presence over the nine younger men in a circle about him.

"As you know," he said, "the NVA's Tenth Division is on the way to Dalat and Lien. They were ambushed along the way, but they should arrive in Dalat tomorrow. Maybe they'll be here in Lien day after tomorrow."

"What should we do to get ready for their coming?" one of the squatting young men asked.

"We'll do nothing. The local militia will melt away before the NVA marches in here. The word has come down that we're not to alienate the local population by killing prominent members. They were not pleased with the death of the pastor."

"The pastor worked with our enemies, the Montagnards. Why were they not pleased?" Tham asked.

"They want us to be known as liberators. After we're in power, the party will, in due time, take care of those who have been our strong enemies. Now go home, rest up, and get ready to celebrate our total victory."

Minh did not return home to rest. He got his bicycle and rode into town. Going by the inn, he looked over the taxis parked in front then continued on to the garage. He got off his bike and walked to the back where his informants slept.

He called their names. They came out of their small room. "When is the American leaving?" Minh asked.

"Sometime tomorrow. Maybe tomorrow night. Mai is going with him. Hal and his family are going in the other taxi."

"Get out as early as possible, and try to find out when they are leaving. I'll come tomorrow morning before daybreak and wait in your room. Tham will be with me. We'll have our AK-47s. We will kill the American before he leaves. Remember we don't want to hurt anyone else."

Minh left as abruptly as he had come. The two young men went back to bed.

Just as he had said, Minh, with his partner, Tham, returned to the small room behind the garage before daybreak with their AK-47s wrapped in burlap sacks because they didn't want any confrontation with the local militia. He gave the two young men some money.

"Get yourselves some noodle soup. Then bring me and Tham some soup and coffee."

When the two young men returned with the soup and coffee, Minh barked to them like a general. "Now get out and find out what's going on. We'll be waiting here. Find out when the American is leaving. He must not get out of town alive."

The two felt pressured, so they tipped their hand. But as it was, they asked too many questions and said too much to another teen with a similar background. That young man, who worked at a bicycle shop, was an acquaintance of Harry's. He told Harry that Minh and a friend were in town waiting for an opportunity to kill his American friend. Harry said nothing about the news and pretended it was not of concern to him, but as soon as the young man had gone, he raced back to the inn.

Bursting into the dining room, he saw John, Hal, and his family drinking tea and talking. "John, Hal, I hear bad news. Bad, bad, no good."

"What is it? What's the bad news?"

"Minh. Minh here in town with friend. They want to kill you, John. They wait behind garage. John must go. Must leave soon, okay?"

Hal talked in Vietnamese with Harry to get all the details. Then he explained things to John.

"Minh and a friend are in a room behind the garage waiting until you go out from the inn. They've sent the two boys who work at the garage to find out the time you're planning on leaving town. They will try to kill you as you come out to get in the taxi."

"It's sad that Minh hates me just because I'm an American. I've never said a word to him."

"That's not the only reason, John. He hates you because you love Mai and are planning on marrying her." Then he added, "I have an idea."

"What is it?"

"Let's get Harry to go back in town and spread the word that you're leaving at four o'clock this evening. But we will leave about two o'clock. When Harry gets through spreading the word in town, he can go out to Mai's house and tell her to be ready to leave at two o'clock. You can go by and get Mai, and we can continue down Highway Twenty to Saigon. We may get inside the ARVN cordon before dark. How about that, John?"

"That's a good idea. I'll be ready."

Hal explained their new plan to Harry in Vietnamese. A grin broke over Harry's face. "Okay, okay, okay," he said. "Harry go now to tell news over town. Harry tell Mai other news."

Chuckling to himself, Harry went out to spread the false rumor. He then would go to the Tuan's house. This would also give him the opportunity to say good-bye to Mai.

Hal cautioned Mrs. Dao to keep the doors locked. If for some reason Minh decided to come to the inn to kill John, he wouldn't get in until they had time to hide in the secret room.

29

Forest Near Dalat

After decimating the NVA platoon with their ambush, Captain Thong and his guerrilla band melted back into the forest. They double-timed back to their base camp. While the troops were resting, Captain Thong congratulated them.

"Men, each of you carried out your assignments very well. Therefore, the ambush was a success. We suffered no casualties. But we cannot rest on our success. Remember, we're guerrillas. We must keep on the move and hit the enemy where they least expect us."

Captain Thong took a drink from his canteen.

"When the NVA remove the bombed trucks from the highway and retrieve their dead and wounded, they will move out to reach Dalat before nightfall. Two of our scouts are watching them."

"We're giving them a dose of their own medicine, aren't we, Captain?" Lieutenant Giang said.

"Yes, and we're going to give them another dose. Lieutenant Tra, I want you to take your men and position yourselves three kilometers up the highway. They'll not be expecting us to hit them again. Empty your magazines on the last two trucks and race back here."

No sooner had Thong finished speaking than the two Montagnard scouts emerged from the forest and quickly approached him. He spoke with them for a few minutes.

"The Tenth is getting ready to move out for Dalat," he said to Tra. "Double-time your troops to the second curve about three kilometers from here. Remember, hit quick and hard and then run."

Twenty minutes after the guerrillas had hurriedly left to set the ambush, Captain Thong, along with his logistics officer and the two scouts who had stayed behind with him, heard the convoy trucks in the distance moving up the highway.

"The Tenth is going to have a big surprise when they get hit again," he told them with a smile.

"Yeah, Captain, and our men are enjoying fighting as guerrillas. For years the Communists have set ambushes for us. Now they're on the receiving end. I'm enjoying it."

"Lieutenant, enjoy it while you can. It will be only a matter of time before the North Vietnamese Army invades Saigon and brings our country under its control. After they have secured the major population centers, they will come after us."

"What are we going to do then, Captain?" asked Lieutenant Giang.

"The only way we can survive," answered Thong, "is to go into Cambodia or get a boat and try to reach another country. But in the meantime, we can harass the NVA and inflict some pain on them for invading our country."

"What other options do we have, Captain?" asked Lieutenant Giang.

"Our options as intelligence officers are very few. We can fight until we die in battle, or we can try to get out of the country. If we are captured or surrender, we will be tortured and shot."

Lieutenant Giang's eyes flashed. "We feel the way you do, Captain. Every one of us is angry with the invading North Vietnamese. We feel ashamed that our army folded so quickly. We want the invaders to know there are some brave fighting men in South Vietnam. They will feel our presence."

"They already have, Lieutenant," Captain Thong responded. "When the men return from the ambush, I want them to camouflage the trucks and hide them as far as possible in the woods. Then we're going to break camp and move two kilometers inland. I want the men to clean up this camp and leave no evidence of our presence."

"Yes sir, Captain. But you know, Captain, when the men return, they will be tired and hungry."

"Yes, we'll eat first. Then we'll change camps. It's not safe for us to stay here any longer. In guerrilla warfare, you can't stay in one place. There are many eyes and ears around us. Because of these ambushes, we will have to keep on the move."

The sound of gunfire in the distance caused the men to pause and listen. They could visualize the ambush, their men firing into the enemy trucks. After a few minutes, the firing stopped. Captain Thong glanced at his watch. He would expect to see his men back in camp in less than forty minutes. He ordered the two scouts to go and make sure no one was following them.

At the expected time, the guerrillas emerged from the forest. They surrounded Captain Thong. Their faces were flushed, and they were breathing heavily, but the adrenalin was flowing, and they carried themselves with the air of victors.

"Captain," Lieutenant Tra reported, "we were in place when the convoy came around the curve. We waited until the last two trucks were in front of us. Their soldiers looked tired and inattentive. We took them by surprise again. Both trucks were wiped out. It was over in less than two minutes, and we were gone."

"Very good. Did you notice any pursuit by the enemy?"

"No, sir. We were moving so fast they had no opportunity to pursue."

"We have two scouts checking out any pursuit. The NVA will not take this second ambush lying down. I won't be surprised if they leave a platoon to stalk us. They don't want their military traffic harassed."

"Captain, my men are ready for any kind of action. But they do need some food and rest now."

"Lieutenant, we're going to eat, and then we'll break camp and move to a new location. After we've eaten, Lieutenant Giang will choose some men to help him camouflage and hide our vehicles in the forest. You take the other men and police the area. Don't leave any evidence of our presence. Then we'll move out to our new base camp."

As the guerrillas were breaking camp, they heard several spasmodic bursts of automatic weapons in the distant forest. Captain Thong wondered if his scouts were involved with the enemy. Just before the guerrillas were leaving the two Montagnard scouts emerged, sweating and breathing heavily. They were quickly taken to Captain Thong.

"Captain, we saw four NVA scouts before they saw us. We got three of them. One escaped. We pursued him toward the highway, but we turned around when we heard him connect with other NVA. Evidently, the Tenth left a number of soldiers here to look for us."

"You men did good work. You're our eyes and ears, and we depend on you. Now you must eat something. We're moving camp."

Captain Thong knew the presence of a number of NVA, possibly a platoon, meant his guerrillas would have to become more mobile if they were to survive. The NVA would increase the numbers according to the resistance.

"We need to live and operate in smaller units," Thong told his lieutenants. "After a few days in our new base camp, we'll begin to operate out of four camps spread out over a wider area. We can hit more targets at different places and keep the NVA off balance."

The new strategy would increase the intensity and effectiveness of the guerrilla forces and their ability to strike more targets at more places, but it would also raise the danger level for them.

30

Sunday, April 6, Road to Saigon

Promptly at two o'clock in the afternoon, John, Mai, Hal, and Hal's family came out of the inn and sped south in their taxis. Harry made sure the word was out all over town that they were to leave at four. John stopped by the Tuan farm to get Mai.

"You go on," he told Hal. "Don't wait for us. We'll not be far behind you."

"Let's meet at the large Catholic church this side of Bien Hoa," Hal said through the car window. "From there, we can go into Saigon together."

Mai was ready to go. She had already said the customary parting words to her parents and siblings. John quickly loaded her suitcase into the car, and they sped off for Saigon.

Ten kilometers down the Saigon highway, John said, "Hal drives like a taxi driver. We'll not see him again until we come to Bien Hoa." But after seventy kilometers, John was surprised to see Hal coming back toward Lien. His family was in the car with him.

Hal flashed his lights and waved at them to stop. He leaned out of the window with a flushed face. "John, the Viet Cong have barricaded the highway. You follow me back to Lien. We must hurry. This road is dangerous now."

It was dark when they arrived back at the inn. They heard that Minh and his friend believed Harry's rumor and came at 3:30 p.m. After learning that John and Mai were gone, Minh and his friend went home. John was relieved that he did not have to worry about Minh in this tense situation. He thought Minh was out of the picture. But that was wishful thinking.

Minh's goal to kill John was an obsession that overrode all common sense and drove him to ignore commands given by the Viet Cong not to kill any more local people. Although Minh never met or talked to John personally, he hated him because he embodied America's presence. He represented what was to Minh the evil, dominating foreign power that attempted to impose its will on the Vietnamese people.

Not only did Minh hate John because he was an American, but also because he came to take Mai back to America. Minh was determined not to allow John to marry Mai. He must kill him.

Minh had left the inn in a rage. But when he cooled off, he began to think more clearly about John's efforts to reach Saigon. He said to Tham, "The American and Hal may not get through to Saigon. I've heard our comrades are setting up roadblocks between here and Saigon."

"Ya, that's true. A number of cars from Dalat and Lien have been turned back."

"Tham, let's go back to the garage. Who knows? They may return to the inn tonight."

After Minh and Tham set up in the room behind the garage, they sent the young men out to watch the inn. "You let us know if you see the taxis return," Minh commanded. "You stay awake and report any activity. Now go!"

An hour after dark, the lookouts ran back to the garage room. "They're back. Both taxis came back. The American, Mai, Hal and family all went back into the inn."

"Good job. Now go back and keep a lookout until we get there. If they come out, get here fast."

Minh and Tham unwrapped their AK-47's. They loaded their magazines.

"Let's go," Minh said. "He won't get away this time. We'll stay as long as it takes to kill the American. Remember, we don't want to shoot anyone besides the American, understand?"

Minh and Tham walked at the edge of the street until they came to the inn. They sent the lookouts back to the garage and stationed themselves across the street.

"Let's keep a lookout for the militia," Minh whispered. "We don't want to have a shootout with them now."

After John, Mai, Hal, and his family had eaten Harry's bean soup with bread and cheese, they discussed their options. They decided to go to Saigon through Phan Rang on the coastal route. They would leave at two o'clock in the morning.

"I know all the back roads," Hal assured John and Mai. "We'll stay away from the NVA coming up from the coast."

Mrs. Dao and Harry advised them to wait in the secret room. Thirty minutes before their departure, Harry would go out and scout around the inn to make sure all was safe.

John sat back to back with Hal listening to his snoring. He thought about his arrival more than a month before and all that happened since. It seemed he had been in Vietnam forever. He glanced at his watch. It was time to leave. He nudged Hal.

"It's time to go. Hal, time to go. Come on. Wake up."

Hal sat up and yawned. "Time to go?"

They climbed the steps out of the secret room. Hal carried his sleeping five-year-old son. The three other children climbed up with Thu, Hal's wife.

"Harry slipped out the side door," Mrs. Dao said. "He is looking around to make sure Minh and his friends are not lurking outside."

Just then Harry returned. "All okay," he said. "You go fast. Harry and Dao pray for you."

Harry had failed to see Minh and Tham. They saw him and stepped into the shadows against the wall across from the inn. Minh and Tham watched Hal load a few extra things into his taxi. Minh carefully pushed his weapon's safety off. John would come out next.

A militia patrol walked down the middle of the street. Hal greeted the men in the patrol.

"Is everything quiet tonight?"

"Ya, everything is quiet." One of the men asked, "Where are you going this time of night?"

"We're going out of town to visit relatives."

"You are not afraid to be out?"

"Naw, the VC never attack taxis. Some of their people use them."

The patrol members all laughed. "We never thought about it that way," they said.

Minh and Tham hugged the wall. John and Mai came out and got into their taxi. Unknowingly, the patrol shielded them from a quick shot by Minh and Tham. Hal and his family climbed into their taxi. They waved to the patrol and sped off into the night.

John and Mai followed Hal. After being briefly stopped by the local militia at the barricade on the edge of town, they were allowed to go on their way. They took the shortcut to avoid going through Dalat. It would intersect with Highway 11 thirty kilometers down from Dalat.

Hal drove like most taxi drivers—fast. John was not used to maneuvering small roads at high speeds, but he kept close behind Hal. Three kilometers from Highway 11, they came upon a barricade and a number of soldiers. The men surrounded Hal's taxi, and several came toward John's car.

"Pray for Hal as he talks with the soldiers," John whispered to Mai.

One of the soldiers motioned for John to get out of his taxi. He spoke to John in English. "You're an American?"

"Yes, I am."

"Your friend told us you want to take your girlfriend to America."

"Yes, I want to marry her and take her to my home," John replied, wondering what was going to happen to them.

"You don't need to be afraid," he said. "We're special forces with the South Vietnamese Army. We're stopping all cars going to Highway Eleven because there are North Vietnamese on the highway."

"Thanks. We're glad you stopped us."

"They will arrest you and take your vehicles. We will show you a shortcut that will take you down three kilometers from the village of Song on Highway Eleven."

"Do you think we can make it to Saigon?" John asked.

"May God help you get to Phan Rang, but I don't think you can make it to Saigon. Thousands of NVA are on Highway One. You will never make it to Saigon."

"Thank you very much, Captain. You speak English well."

"Yes, many of us were trained by the Americans. Actually, I'm a lieutenant. My captain speaks very good English. He's married to an American. She just returned to Texas."

"Texas is my home also."

"Here comes my captain now. Captain, this man is an American trying to get his girlfriend out of Vietnam. They want to go to the coast."

Captain Thong bent down and looked into the car. "John Gunter! I'm glad to see you again. The situation is dangerous, but I think you can make it to the coast."

"Thanks, Captain. We're going for it."

"I advised your Vietnamese friend you should try to get a boat at Phan Rang and escape by sea; otherwise you will never make it out of Vietnam. Now you should go so you can get down the mountain before daybreak. May God go with you."

Captain Thong and his men directed Hal and John to a back road a hundred meters from the barricade.

The rough road was barely passable, so John and Hal were forced to drive slowly as they maneuvered around holes and other obstacles. Daylight was breaking when they arrived at the village of Song on Highway 11. Feeling solid pavement beneath their wheels, they sped toward Phan Rang.

Coming into the village of Ninh Son, Hal stopped in front of a small cafe. He got out and walked back to talk to John.

"I know the people in this café," he said. "I've eaten here many times. They will give us good information about Phan Rang. Let's get something to eat while we're here, but we must hurry."

While Hal talked to the middle-aged couple that owned the café, their helpers prepared noodle soup and boiled eggs for the early customers. They quickly ate breakfast. Hal, between mouthfuls, repeated what the couple had told him.

"They said we'll never make it into Phan Rang on this highway. There are too many NVA along the way. They advised us to take a back road just past the Cham Temples that will take us into Phan Rang."

"Where are we going in Phan Rang?" Mai asked.

"They gave us the name of a small café. We can hide our taxis there. They will put us in contact with people who will help us get a boat."

Back in his taxi, John wondered how many more narrow escapes lay ahead of them. But the desire to escape to freedom was greater than the anxiety of getting out of the country.

31

Sunday, April 6, Mountains Near Dalat

Captain Thong met with his three officers. "Men, one of the rules of guerrilla warfare is to hit fast and hard and get out of there. This is why we're going to divide up into four units of twenty plus men in each unit."

"How far apart are we going to be Captain?" Lieutenant Tra asked.

"We're going to be around twenty kilometers apart. Lieutenant, you'll be south of Highway Eleven from the shortcut road to Lien and Dalat. Lieutenant Giang you'll be fifty kilometers down near the village of Song and Lieutenant Dang you'll be all the way down to the foot of the mountain. I will be north of Highway Eleven near Dalat."

The NVA platoon left behind by the Tenth Division was a thorn in the flesh to the guerrillas. They sent out patrols every day and night keeping the guerrillas off balance. The NVA lost five men in firefights while the guerrillas lost two. Captain Thong's strategy of spreading his men over a larger area made it more difficult for the NVA.

Lieutenant Giang's men ambushed a small convoy coming up the mountain near the village of Song. Only twelve soldiers guarded the convoy of cars and small trucks composed mostly of NVA officers. The convoy was almost completely wiped out. This ambush frustrated the Tenth Division Commanders and especially the platoon leaders who were given the responsibility of protecting vehicles on Highway 11.

Just hours after Giang's ambush, Captain Thong's unit attacked two trucks from Dalat bringing supplies to the platoon left to guard the highway. The two trucks were destroyed, and ten of the fifteen soldiers were killed. The captain and his forces slipped back into the forest without any killed or wounded.

The Tenth's commander, General Than, was enraged when he received word of the two attacks on Highway 11. He wiped the sweat from his brow and paced around his command center located in the Dalat Palace Hotel overlooking Xuan Huong Lake.

Glaring at two of his subordinates, he ranted, "One of the two trucks was attacked just ten kilometers from here. Enough is enough! I want a platoon of our rangers sent to take out those insurgents. Now!"

General Dung had already sent a message to General Than chiding him for being so slow in moving the Tenth toward Saigon. He even jibed that the colonel must be enjoying Dalat so much he was reluctant to leave it.

General Than knew General Dung wasn't joking. He was intimating that he expected the Tenth to move out of Dalat. But these latest attacks would further slow the Tenth's movement. The normally easygoing General Than was feeling the pressure of the commander's short fuse.

Captain Thong's plan to harass and slow down the NVA was working, but he knew their days were numbered. He realized their continued attacks on the NVA would arouse them to send more troops to find and engage them in the mountains.

His assessment of the NVA's response to the guerrilla's attacks was accurate. The Tenth's crack platoon of rangers intended to search out and destroy the guerrillas. The level of opposition was raised to a new and dangerous level for the four units operating under Captain Thong's command. In order to survive, they would have to stay on the move, strike fast, and run.

The two Montagnard scouts reported to Captain Thong about the ranger platoon.

"Captain, this new platoon is the NVA's best fighting unit. They are hardened veterans and very aggressive. They will come after us and keep coming until they engage us. We encountered their scouts and barely escaped. We pinned them down for a moment and then made a run for it."

"Do you think they followed you to our camp?"

"No. We set an ambush in case they got onto our trail. We didn't see them again, but they're looking for us."

"You did well. You're two of the best scouts in Vietnam. Now you need to eat and rest up. We're moving out in an hour."

Captain Thong was not going to sit around and wait for the NVA to engage his guerrillas. He had a plan, and he was immediately moving out to set his plan in motion. If the NVA wanted to meet them, then they would but on the guerrillas' terms.

The two Montagnard scouts were sent ahead to notify the lieutenants of their roles in the plan while Captain Thong and his unit went deeper inland from the highway. They set a course that would take them back to their original base camp. There they set about getting the camouflaged trucks out of the forest and ready for action.

Several men were sent to Sergeant Huy's village to scrounge up all the North Vietnamese helmets and caps they could find. They only procured fifteen, but that would be enough for the truck drivers and a few soldiers to give the appearance of being North Vietnamese troops.

Captain Thong and his unit spent the night three kilometers inland from their original base camp. He wasn't taking any chance of being surprised by the NVA. He knew they were aggressively looking for them.

Lieutenant Giang's unit was due to join them at nine the following morning. Giang would take one truck, and Thong would take another for their venture up the mountain.

Shortly after eight, Lieutenant Giang and his men arrived at the base camp. They had left the village of Song just after midnight and traveled mostly along the highway. But several times they had skirted inland to avoid NVA troops. Tired from their early morning march, they needed an hour's rest before they boarded the truck for their forage into enemy territory.

At nine thirty, the two trucks loaded with the guerrilla units pulled out. With their helmets and caps, they looked as much like North Vietnamese as possible. Captain Thong knew the NVA was using many captured ARVN vehicles, so their trucks would not be conspicuous. The guerrillas were to keep their M-16s out of sight as much as possible.

"If the NVA soldiers greet you," he instructed, "answer in a friendly manner using the North Vietnamese dialect. If they ask who you are, tell them you're replacements for the Tenth Division."

Five kilometers up the mountain they saw ten NVA soldiers patrolling the highway. The Northern soldiers waved and smiled as the two trucks passed. Sitting in the cab of the lead truck, Captain Thong smiled at the waving soldiers.

"Sergeant, we're fooling them so far," he said to the driver. "They cannot imagine that we would dare come up this mountain in a truck and ride into their very headquarters. That's guerrilla warfare, Sergeant. You do what they least expect. Let's hope we fool the others on the way to our target."

"Let's hope so, Captain. Our daring to drive up to their very headquarters will catch them off guard. But it will be like stirring up a hornets' nest."

"Yes, you're right. We'll hit them so fast and hard they won't know what's happening. By the time they recover, we'll be flying back down the mountain to get out of the hornets' nest."

General Than had risen through the ranks to command the Tenth Division. His sturdy build, barrel chest and deep voice were perfect qualities for military leadership. His round, bulldog-like face gave the impression that he was a determined, tenacious man. His staff sat stiffly in their chairs while General Than, as was his habit, paced around the room.

"Men, I just heard from General Dung. He said we're needed in the battle at Xuan Loc. When the battle there is won, the victors will march into Saigon." He stopped and faced his staff. "I would like the Tenth to march into Saigon, wouldn't you?"

A chorus responded, "Yes, yes, we would."

"General Dung asked me if our area here was secured," General Than continued. "I told him yes except for some bands of guerrillas. He told me, 'Take care of them and get on down here to Xuan Loc.'"

He turned to Major Quang. "Major, what about that company of rangers we sent to take out the guerrillas? What have they done?"

"Their scouts have had skirmishes with some of the guerrillas. They're looking for their base camp and an opportunity to hit their main body. I think we have them on the run."

"You think they're on the run? That's what guerrillas do. They run here and there, and they hit us when and where least expected. I don't want them on the run. I want them eliminated."

"Yes sir, General. I'll send word to the company commander to take care of business and do it soon."

"Soon can't be too soon. They've hit us ten kilometers from our headquarters. That's not acceptable. Now staff, I want the Tenth to secure this area and to do it soon. I want us in the thick of the fight at Xuan Loc, and I want to lead the Tenth into Saigon. Now, let's get to it."

General Than and his staff were about to experience something they could not even envision.

32

Sunday, April 6, Phan Rang

At the same time Captain Thong's two trucks dared to drive up the mountain into the NVA headquarters at Dalat, the two taxis left the cafe at Vinh Son and drove toward Phan Rang. They passed the Cham Temples and veered right onto an unpaved road that took them to the outskirts of Phan Rang. The potholes in the road forced them to drive slowly.

Hal kept a lookout for the *Que Huong* (hometown) cafe. Just as they approached the city limits of Phan Rang, it came into view. It was not much to look at with its outside boards faded and bleached by years of sun and rain. Directly behind the cafe two small houses resembled the cafe with their outside bleached boards.

The taxis parked behind the cafe. Hal motioned that he would go in alone. Minutes later he came out with a middle-aged man. The man motioned to John and Hal to move their taxis behind the two small houses.

Then he took them into one of the buildings and told them it would be their living quarters until he could locate a boat for them.

There was just enough space to bed down on straw mats at night. During the day, the mats would be rolled up and stood in a corner.

While the others unloaded the taxis, Hal and the cafe owner talked about the needed boat. Several times they both raised their voices and almost shouted at one another. Then they would moderate their voices and talk in low tones. When they finished bargaining, Hal came in the house to share the results of the conversation.

"The man is demanding twice what the boat is worth," Hal told John, "because he knows you're an American. He wants two thousand dollars for an old twenty-foot fishing boat."

Both Mai and Thu made hissing sounds that expressed their disgust about the high price.

"What did you say?" John asked.

"I told him I would give him the two taxis for the boat. He said, 'The North Vietnamese will take the taxis from me, and I'll get in trouble because of them. No, I don't want the taxis.' Then I offered him seven hundred fifty dollars. He laughed and told me to get some rest and then maybe I could talk sensibly."

"It's a shame he wants to take advantage of us in this situation," observed Mai, "but keep on bargaining with him, and he may come down on his price. Not many people could pay two thousand dollars for a boat."

"Yeah, Hal," John added, "I think he's testing you. He will come down on his price."

"Maybe he will. I'm a good bargainer, but time is important. We can't stay here long without been discovered by the military police. You know they're patrolling the area now. Our contact man told me military police caught two groups trying to escape out yesterday."

"Hal, are you sure you can trust this man?" Mai asked nervously. "He may turn us in."

"We can trust him. He wants to get all the money he can from us before we leave the country, but he hates the Communists. We don't need to worry about him betraying us."

"What can we be doing today?" John asked. "Hal, can't you go out and find someone else who wants to sell a boat? You may find a better price. We should try to leave as soon as possible."

Hal shook his head. "We have to be patient. If I go out and start asking about a boat there's a good possibility of someone telling the military police. We need to stay close to the house until we can get a boat. The cafe will bring food here to us, so we don't need to go into the cafe."

"We gotta have some kind of exercise, Hal," John said.

"We can go out after dark and walk around. There's an outlet behind the house where we can get water and take a bird bath."

Mai, Thu, and the children lay down on the straw mats. John and Hal sat near the window discussing their next destination. "We might try the Philippines," Hal said. "They're straight across the South China Sea from here."

"Once we get out in a small boat like that, Hal, we'll be at the mercy of the sea. The wind and waves might take us in any direction. We'll need plenty of drinking water and buckets to bail seawater out of the boat. Our best bet will be to get picked up by some freighter that will take us to one of their countries."

"You may be right. I know there must be hundreds of boats out in the sea filled with people just like us trying to escape Vietnam."

John placed his hand on his friend's shoulder. "We're going to get out, Hal."

"Yes, we must get out of this country. There's no other option." Hal gazed out the window. He exclaimed, "John, there's the military police! They just drove up to the cafe. Let's get away from the window."

Dreading a knock on the door, John and Hal conversed in whispers. After a tense twenty minutes, Hal peeked out carefully. "They're gone. This shows we have to be careful. People are coming here from all parts of Vietnam trying to escape the country.

The police especially want to catch those they consider traitors and enemies to their cause."

"What happens when they catch those they consider traitors?"

"They execute many of them. Others are sent off to hard labor prisons."

"No wonder they're trying to escape." John paused. "How about us, Hal? What would they do if they caught us?"

"They'd probably send me to hard labor since I'm trying to escape. But you, they would send you to prison, also. But since you're an American, your government would eventually get you out."

John was quiet for several moments. "They're not going to catch us. We'll escape to freedom. I feel it. I'm praying for us to get away, and I trust the Lord to deliver us. Hal, do you believe in the Lord God?"

"Yes, I do, John. Maybe, not as strong as you do, but I've been praying a lot here lately. You know I am a Catholic. Maybe not a good Catholic, but I do believe and pray. And I talked with Pastor Chanh."

"Did you often talk with him?"

"Yes. When I talked with him, something always moved in my heart. I wept for him when I heard the Communists killed him. He was such a great man of God. And even now when I think of him, my heart moves and tears come to my eyes."

"I know how you feel. I really loved Pastor Chanh. He meant a lot to my life, and my heart hurts when I think of him and his family left behind."

With the coming of darkness, Hal encouraged everyone to go outside and walk in the vacant lot behind the two houses. "Don't walk on the road in front of the café," he warned. "Military police patrol the road. And anytime you see a car coming, get behind the houses."

John and Mai played games with Hal's four children on the vacant lot in the faint moonlight. The children's laughter reminded them of evenings in a typical Vietnamese village. It was near midnight when they returned to the room to sleep.

At daybreak there was a banging on the door. Hal groggily got up to open the door. It was the contact man. He spoke in a low, urgent voice.

"I just got word that the police are checking houses near the beach. You need to go now. Park your taxis behind the chicken house. That's the building on the other side of the vacant lot. I'll take you to my sister's house. She lives three hundred meters from here."

They carefully picked up their belongings, rolled the straw mats, and placed them in the corner. John and Hal took their things to the taxis and locked them in the trunk then drove behind the rickety old chicken house. They followed the contact man to his older sister's house.

She welcomed them with a toothless smile. Her husband had been dead ten years, and her only two sons killed in the war. She was the only survivor in her family. So she sold her house in Phan Thiet and moved to Phan Rang to be near her brother. She lived alone for several years and, typical of those who live alone, enjoyed talking when she had the opportunity.

Her face lit at the sight of the children. "How about breakfast?" She began to prepare noodles, boiled eggs, and coffee.

Mai and Thu joined her in the kitchen. She talked incessantly while Mai and Thu sprinkled the conversation with, "Ya, ya, ya," to acknowledge that they were listening.

After breakfast, the contact man led the travelers back to the house. "My informant was right," he told them. "Police came and looked in the house. They seemed to be satisfied that no one was here. But you must get out as soon as possible. It's not good for you or for me for you to be here. If they catch you in my house, I'm in bad trouble."

Before returning to the café, he told Hal, "I'll be back later to talk about the boat."

"Hal, whatever it takes," John said, "We've gotta get a boat and get outta here."

"Tomorrow I'll close out the deal with this man. We can't stay here much longer without getting arrested by the Communist."

33

On the way into Dalat, the two-truck convoy met scattered groups of soldiers patrolling the highway. Thinking they were replacements, the soldiers waved and smiled at the guerrillas.

The trucks rolled to a stop at a barricade five kilometers from Dalat. Captain Thong and the guerrillas were tense. They had not anticipated a barricade. An NVA lieutenant came up to the lead truck. Captain Thong leaned out the window and greeted him in the North Vietnamese dialect.

"Hello, Lieutenant. We're replacements for the Tenth. We were supposed to have reported yesterday. You know the army, always a day late."

The lieutenant smiled. "Ya, that's right. Say, can you take one of my men to Dalat? He's got a horrible toothache and needs to see a dentist."

"I would be glad to, Lieutenant, but we are packed full. If the men aren't in a space, then that space is taken up with our equipment. Sorry, Lieutenant. We're late. We need to report as soon as possible."

The NVA lieutenant hesitated a moment and then waved the trucks through the barricade. As they pulled through, Captain Thong alerted the driver, "Sergeant, look over the barricade carefully."

While they drove on toward Dalat, Captain Thong asked, "Do you think we can ram through the barricade with the trucks?"

"Yes, Captain. There are only five men at the post. When we come back through, they may not know about our activity in Dalat. We can take them out quickly and remove the barricade. If we ram the barricade, it could damage the trucks."

"Very good, Sergeant." Captain Thong was pleased.

They came into Dalat near the east end of Xuan Huong Lake. Captain Thong's trained military eye saw the outpost garrisoned by forty to fifty soldiers. He knew they would have to be the first target. As they passed the outpost, the unsuspecting NVA soldiers waved at them.

The trucks continued up the road a hundred meters until they found a place to turn around. Then at moderate speed they drove back toward the outpost. They approached with rifle safety controls off.

When the lead truck was alongside the outpost, without stopping, the shooters poured a barrage of fire into it. The NVA soldiers were completely taken by surprise. Soldiers left standing were taken out by shooters in the second truck.

As soon as the trucks had passed the stricken outpost, they sped down the mountain gathering speed as they went and shooting at startled NVA soldiers along the highway. Arriving back at the barricade, the five unsuspecting soldiers were taken out by auto rifle fire. Four guerrillas jumped down and removed the barricades and then replaced them behind the trucks. That would slow down any pursuing vehicles.

The two trucks roared down the mountain leaving a confused and angry division in their wake. But the guerrillas' mission was not finished. There were NVA soldiers all along the way, and they could be hit in passing.

Ten kilometers from Dalat, the trucks came upon twenty NVA along the highway. Captain Thong saw a number of rangers on the edge of the forest down from the large group. He immediately sensed the danger, but his shooters were already pouring fire into the startled main group.

The small group of battle-hardened rangers, unshaken, began to fire at the trucks. Captain Thong crouched as low in his seat as possible as bullets slammed into the windshield between him and the driver. The guerrilla shooters could return fire until the trucks were beside the rangers' position. A burst of fire from an AK-47 went through the driver's side window and caught the sergeant in the chest.

Captain Thong heard the horrible impact of the bullets and the gasping for air of the wounded sergeant. He quickly grabbed the wheel to steer the careening truck while moving the fatally wounded sergeant to the floorboard of the passenger side.

The two trucks roared on down the mountain, but Captain Thong knew they were bloodied in the exchange of fire. Lieutenant Tra and Lieutenant Dang set up units to ambush any vehicles that followed the trucks.

Before they could reach the original base camp, Captain Thong knew they were to go through the first platoon left on the highway by the Tenth. He grimaced at the partly shattered windshield. Small groups of soldiers from the first platoon stood idly beside the highway. He heard bursts of fire from their M-16s, but he didn't slow down or look back. For the next five kilometers, his men blasted away at the NVA soldiers. Those not hit scattered into the woods like startled chickens.

The convoy came to the road that led to Sergeant Huy's village and pulled off two hundred meters into the forest. When they checked their causalities, Captain Thong saw that his unit had been hit the hardest since the lead truck had taken the brunt of the rangers' fire. Two men were dead and three wounded, one seriously. In the second truck, Lieutenant Giang's unit suffered one dead and two slightly wounded.

Captain Thong sent ten of his men back along the village road to set an ambush for anyone who might follow them into the forest. The dead and wounded were taken into the village. There were several medical people there to help. The dead would be buried later when the guerillas were sure there was no enemy activity in the area.

At the edge of the village, Captain Thong sat on a straw mat with Lieutenant Giang. Two women brought them hot tea and sweet biscuits. For several minutes, the two guerrilla officers said nothing. The younger officer could see the tiredness in the eyes of his commander. The lines in his face seemed deeper nowadays. Lieutenant Giang spoke first.

"Captain, that was a brilliant move. We took the NVA by surprise. It'll spread confusion in their camp."

"Yes, but they'll come with more force and determination now. We'll have to plan our next moves carefully. Our time is limited, so we must make every day count."

The captain's prediction was even more accurate than he could envision.

34

April 7–8, Phan Rang

Hal and John's contact knocked on the door of the house behind the restaurant. Hal answered the door and went outside to talk with him. The conversation lasted more than thirty minutes as the men bargained back and forth about the price of the boat.

Hal came back and motioned to John.

"The man has come down to seven hundred dollars. I don't think he'll come down any more. What do you think?"

"Good job, Hal. Let's go for it!"

"He wants American dollars. Can you pay half in US dollars?"

"Sure. Let's close the deal."

"Here's what we'll do, John. You give me two hundred dollars for earnest money. We'll pay him the rest when we get the boat."

"When will he get it?" John asked, taking two bills from his money belt.

"He'll meet us at three o'clock tomorrow morning on a deserted beach about a kilometer to the north. I've instructed him to put plenty of water and food in the boat. He wants twenty-five dollars more for that."

"Very good. Here's the money to take care of that now."

"He'll be pleased. I believe he will deliver. Today we need to make our preparations and get as much rest as we can for the trip."

The man's wife and daughter brought breakfast to the hopeful escapees. While they were eating, Hal explained the plans for the day.

"We'll prepare what we need to take with us. Everything unnecessary must be left behind. We want to keep the boat as light as possible."

"What time will we go?" Mai asked.

"We'll leave the house at two o'clock and walk to the north beach a kilometer away. The road patrolled by the military police is about two hundred meters from the beach. We'll hide on this side of the beach road until time to get into the boat."

"Who will close out the deal with the contact man?" Mai asked.

"I will dress as a fisherman and go alone to close the deal. If the police come by during that time, they will think we are fishermen. When the boat is ready, I will come and get the rest of you."

Mai, Thu, and the children talked in low tones as they made last minute preparations. They felt a sense of joyful relief but also underlying tension.

John and Hal went to the taxis and got their baggage from the trunk. They sorted through their belongings, keeping only what they deemed necessary for the trip. Several times Hal exhorted Thu and the children to cut back on what they wanted to take. They were on the verge of tears several times as Hal said, "No, no, you don't need that. When we get to America, I will buy you a dozen of them."

Hal's stern tone combined with his good-natured bantering and promises brought his family through the trauma of parting with most of their clothes and other coveted items. John kept a jacket and baseball cap. Mai had a basketball-sized bundle of her belongings.

Both John and Hal wore money belts inside their clothing. John had twenty-five hundred US dollars, and Hal had seven thousand. During the last weeks, he had taken a number of rich Vietnamese families to Saigon and other coastal cities, and they paid him well. Thu also owned a considerable amount of gold jewelry.

The group ate an early evening meal and tried to rest. The children finally fell asleep while Mai and Thu talked for hours. John and Hal sat in a corner and talked past midnight before they dozed off sitting up.

John woke with a start. Someone was knocking softly on the door. It took a few seconds for him to realize where he was. Hal snored quietly. John shook Hal's shoulder.

"Hal, someone is at the door. Wake up and answer the door."

"Who? What—what is it?" Hal muttered groggily.

"Someone is at the door," John repeated. "You need to answer."

Hal slowly stood and opened the door just a crack. He saw the contact man and stepped outside to converse with him in undertones.

When he came back in the house, he was wide awake.

"John, the police suspect something. They're raiding houses near the beach. We've got to move fast. We'll go to his sister's house. Let's get everyone up."

Hal woke Thu and his older children while John woke Mai. She helped Thu with the younger children. Hal and John took their provisions and baggage to the nearby chicken house. They rolled up the mats and placed them in the corner.

The man led them to his sister's house. She greeted them in a whisper, again smiling broadly. She helped Mai and Thu put the children down for the rest of the night. The two younger ones had never awakened.

"You can't go tonight, of course," the man told them. "Maybe tomorrow night. The person who warned me said the police caught two groups tonight trying to get out by boat. It's dangerous for you and for me." He paused at the door. "Stay here until I come for you."

At daybreak, he came to tell Hal they could go back to the beach house. "Move out early," he urged, "before people start moving about."

The widow gave Hal and John a cup of coffee while Mai and Thu awakened the children. She had prepared noodles and boiled eggs for them to take back to the beach house. After reaching their house, they ate, unrolled the mats, and settled down to rest again. John and Hal left their belongings in the chicken house in case they had to move out on a moment's notice.

Just before noon the contact man dropped by. "You can leave tonight," he told Hal. "We'll follow the same plan at the same time and the same place. Stay in the house, and be ready to leave quickly if I hear the police are coming."

Early that evening, the man's wife and daughter brought food and hot tea. The group felt refreshed after devouring the food. After dark, John and Mai took the children outside to get some exercise. Mai, Thu, and the children settled down at ten o'clock. John and Hal talked until half past eleven and finally drifted off to sleep.

John knew he would have the responsibility to get Hal up. Hal was a sound sleeper, while John slept lightly. Later he woke with a start. It took a few seconds for him to orient himself. Hal was snoring. Glancing at his watch, he saw it was one thirty.

He felt relieved he had awakened in time. What if they had all overslept and missed their opportunity to escape? Listening to Hal's deep, sound snoring he knew Hal would never have awakened on his own. John decided to let him sleep fifteen minutes more.

Mai and Thu were already awake. They woke the children gently as only women can when they know a long, dangerous trip lies ahead.

"Go quietly and stay together," Hal whispered. "We'll cross the main road and walk toward the beach. Let's walk on this side of the beach road until we come to a shanty with old boats around it. You will wait there hidden among the boats until I come and get you."

Hal put a bandana around his head. He wore trousers cut off at the knees and rubber flops. Even though the situation was serious, Hal's children giggled at their father's appearance. He always looked sharp and modern. To see him dressed like a fisherman brought them to the verge of laughter.

The group cautiously moved across the road and came to the shanty. John, with the women and children, hid among some abandoned fishing boats. Hal continued down to the seashore. Only a few minutes after he left, John saw the lights of a vehicle coming down the beach road. It must be the military police.

"Stay down, and be very quiet," John whispered.

The truck stopped in front of the shanty about thirty meters from the road. John's heart was pounding. Would they be caught now? A feeling of despair swept through him.

Two soldiers got out of the truck and walked toward the beach. "What are you doing there this time of the morning?" they hollered to the café owner.

"Getting our boat ready to go out," he called back. "We can't make a living staying in bed all night with our wives, can we?"

The two soldiers laughed and then turned, got back into their jeep, and continued down the road.

In five more minutes, Hal came and took everyone to the waiting boat. John and Hal pulled it into shallow water and helped the women and children aboard. They shook hands with their contact and climbed into the boat. As Hal predicted, he delivered on what he promised. He called to the escapees, "God be with you!"

As the boat pulled away from the shores of Vietnam, John said, "With the Lord's help, we did it."

Mai joined in. "Praise the Lord, He saved us and made a way for us."

Hal hugged Thu and the children. In the faint moonlight, John saw tears running down his cheeks.

John remembered it was now April the eighth. He had been in Vietnam forty days. It seemed an eternity to him. As the twenty-foot fishing boat chugged out on the expansive sea, he knew uncertain and dangerous days lay ahead.

35

April 9, Lien Road

"Trucks dropped the platoon of North Vietnamese soldiers seven kilometers from the Dalat-Phan Rang highway. The North Vietnamese scouts came across Lieutenant Tra's guerrillas returning from an attempted ambush. The three scouts quickly hid themselves and followed the twenty guerrillas to where they made camp for the coming night and then hurried back to report to their lieutenant.

The lieutenant decided to move into position to attack the guerrillas as they were relaxing, ready to bed down for the night. In late afternoon, they quietly moved three hundred meters from the enemy camp.

Lieutenant Tra sent scouts to patrol the area between their camp and the Dalat-Phan Rang highway, but he made a tactical error in not patrolling the Lien road. He would pay dearly for that mistake.

The guerrillas finished eating just before dusk. Some were cleaning their weapons, and others were lounging in small groups when the NVA platoon opened fire. The first barrage took out ten of the guerrillas, including Lieutenant Tra. The remaining eight grabbed their weapons, jumped behind trees, and returned fire. Knowing they were outnumbered, they retreated into the forest, moving from tree to tree, covering one another as they ran to escape. They joined their two scouts and set up an ambush in case they were followed.

The next morning, the surviving guerrillas from Lieutenant Tra's unit limped back down the mountain to the original base camp to unite with Captain Thong's unit. Two of the guerrillas had been wounded and needed medical attention.

Saddened by the loss of so many of his men, Captain Thong questioned the surviving guerrillas about every detail of the ambush.

"Where did the enemy forces come from?"

"They must have come from Lien, Captain. We placed two scouts out between us and the Dalat-Phan Rang highway."

" No scouts on the Lien road?"

"No, sir. There was no enemy activity on that road."

"Lieutenant Tra was a good soldier, God rest his soul, but that was a mistake. We must know where the enemy is on all fronts. But that platoon will pay for that ambush. We'll show them what it's like to be on the receiving end. They should know when you catch a tiger by his tail you will get hurt."

Leaving the two wounded men in the village, Captain Thong and the remaining guerrillas struck out for the Lien road. Counting the eight men from Lieutenant Tra's unit, there were twenty-six guerrillas, including Captain Thong.

The captain sent the two Montagnard scouts to find the platoon's location. "Watch out for their scouts. They'll be looking for us," he warned.

Captain Thong moved his men a kilometer inland from the highway. They secured a place in the thick forest to rest and wait for the scouts' report.

The two Montagnard scouts reported back to Captain Thong late in the evening.

"Captain, we saw their scouts, but they didn't see us. We moved in the forest parallel to the road. Three soldiers walked within three meters of where we were hiding. They were talking about a supply truck coming from Dalat tomorrow. We estimate there are around fifty-five soldiers in the platoon."

"If a supply truck is coming from Dalat, the enemy will send patrols out looking for an ambush, right?"

"Yes, sir, Captain. They will patrol both sides of the highway."

"That's exactly what we would do, Corporal. Good work, men. Get some food and rest. We're moving out early in the morning."

April 10, Mountains Near Dalat

Captain Thong and his men met daylight walking parallel with the Lien road three hundred meters inland. "Keep on the lookout for NVA scouts," he cautioned the two Montagnard scouts. "If you see them, report back to me."

The scouts reported back in an hour. "You were right, Captain. The enemy is patrolling both sides of the Lien road going toward the Dalat-Phan Rang highway. Evidently, their supply truck is coming from that way this morning."

"How far is their base camp from the Dalat-Phan Rang highway?"

"About seven kilometers."

"Is it on the right or left side of the road?"

"It's on the right about two hundred meters inland."

"Would you guess the patrol would ride back after they meet the truck?"

"Captain, if we had already patrolled the road, we would want to ride back."

"I agree. We'll continue toward Lien another two kilometers. You scouts stay at least a hundred meters ahead of us. When we are across from the enemy's base camp, we'll set up and wait for the supply truck."

The North Vietnamese Tenth Division was short on vehicles because the guerrilla ambushes destroyed six of their trucks. The supply sergeant and his squad at Lien did not have a truck available to supply the platoon patrolling the Lien Highway. Dalat took all their trucks. So he requested the platoon be supplied from Dalat. But the supply major in Dalat informed him they were also short on vehicles and told him to procure a truck in Lien.

Since the Communist take-over in Lien, Minh strutted around town trying to ingratiate himself with the new leadership. The NVA leaders, however, had no time for him. When Minh heard they were looking for trucks, he saw an opportunity to put himself in a position of importance. "Sergeant," he said, "I know where you can get some trucks."

"Where?" the sergeant asked. "I drove a truck for a man named Hao. He left town with his family and an American, but he left seven trucks at his in-laws place two kilometers outside Lien."

"Can you take me to the place?"

"Sure, I can."

The supply sergeant and three of his men accompanied Minh to the two-acre plot of the aging couple. Minh knocked on the door.

"Good morning, Mr. and Mrs. Nguyen. Excuse us for disturbing you, but we have come for something important. The liberating army is in bad need of trucks at this time. We know you have seven trucks here, and we need to borrow them to haul supplies."

Looking at the four NVA soldiers with Minh, Mr. Nguyen retorted, "We don't have seven trucks. Hao gave three of them to his drivers. He asked us to take care of the other trucks until we can give them to his brother."

Sensing that Mr. Nguyen did not respect Minh or the NVA, the sergeant stepped forward. "Mr. Nguyen, we can leave you a receipt for the trucks, but we must take them now. As you know, there is a change of government in this province. You and all other citizens must cooperate with us. Now, get us the keys to the trucks."

Mr. Nguyen was not easily intimidated, but he understood it would be better to comply. He went into a back room and returned with the truck keys. The soldiers drove the four trucks back to Lien.

The supply sergeant was elated. Procuring the four trucks would please his superiors.

"Sergeant," Minh said, "Let me drive the truck to supply the platoon. I know the countryside, and I'm used to driving these trucks."

Since Minh had been the source of his good fortune, the sergeant agreed. Shortly after nine, the loaded truck with Minh at the wheel and an accompanying soldier pulled out of Lien to supply the bivouacking platoon. It never entered their minds that there could be an ambush. They felt secure knowing the platoon was patrolling the area.

Anticipating the supply truck from Dalat, Captain Thong and his guerrillas positioned themselves fifty meters from the highway across from the NVA platoon's base camp. He was surprised when one of his scouts came running up to him.

"Captain, the supply truck is coming from Lien."

"Let's set up an ambush near the road," he said. "Wait until as many soldiers as possible are gathered around the truck before you open fire."

The supply truck lumbered up and stopped in the road directly in front of the waiting guerrillas hiding in the forest. The twenty-six guerrillas approached in bent-over position the first twenty-five meters then crawled the remaining distance to the edge of the road with their weapons ready to commence firing.

Just as Captain Thong had projected, twenty soldiers came running to meet the truck. Four climbed into the truck bed to push the supplies to waiting hands on the ground. They were laughing and enjoying the camaraderie of the moment when Thong gave the signal to open fire.

The startled soldiers didn't have a chance to fire back. Only a few of them carried their weapons in hand. It was over in two minutes. No one survived the ambush. Minh lay dead on the edge of the road.

36

South China Sea

John hugged Mai and raised both hands toward heaven. "We did it. We did it. With God's help, we did it." He had escaped the shores of Vietnam with the woman he loved. But that was not his final goal, only a main objective along the way.

The ten-horsepower engine that powered the boat ran evenly as it pushed the boat over the dark water. Two cans of gasoline onboard would last several days. True to his word, their contact packed three large cans of water and food supplies into the boat. By daybreak, the shoreline of Vietnam receded from view. The cool morning breeze stirred small waves that lapped against the boat. The two women and children cuddled down in the middle of the boat and were sound asleep.

"Get some sleep, Hal," John called over the engine noise. "I'll stay at the helm."

Hal nodded and found a place to stretch out. In a few moments, he was fast asleep. John zipped his jacket leaning into the wind. In every direction, he saw nothing but the expansiveness of the sea. He'd enjoy the cool now. Later it was going to get hot.

An hour after sunrise, John could feel the air heating up. The sun woke Hal, Mai, and Thu, but the children continued to sleep. They passed the canteen around. Each person drank a full cup of water to wash down the sardines from the food provisions.

Mai came and sat beside John. They talked, laughed, and leaned against one another as if they were on a honeymoon vacation cruise. Hal and Thu discussed the prospects of their unknown future in America. When the children woke up, they were excited about the adventure of being on a boat in the middle of the sea heading for an unknown shore.

The day passed pleasantly with the excited chatter of the children and the muffled roar of the boat engine. But John knew it was only the first day in the boat out on the South China Sea.

The morning of the second day they came within a hundred meters of another boat. The same size as theirs, it moved slowly under the weight of at least twenty people. The man at the helm called out, "Take some of our people! We're overloaded! Take some of our people!"

"What should we do, Hal?" John asked, feeling the gravity of the situation. "We can take some of them, can't we?"

"John, if we come near their boat, half their people will get into our boat. Then we'll be in the same plight they are. They'll eat all of our food provisions and drink up our water. No, John, I don't think we should take them on board."

Thu agreed. "And we don't know what kind of people we would be taking in. They could be gangsters and try to take over the boat."

"We can hope a ship will take them in soon," Mai added.

They slowly pulled away from the other boat. In his heart, John knew his companions were right in their assessment of the situation. "If we are not picked up by a ship, we'll be out of food, water, and gas in three or four days," he said.

John was right in his projection. On the fourth day, he said to his boat-mates, "We've got to ration the food and water. If we eat and drink just a little each day, our provisions could last three more days."

"What are we going to do, John, when we have no food or water?" Mai asked.

"The only thing we can do is pray like crazy and ask the Lord to send a ship to rescue us."

At the end of the third day of rationing, the food and water were gone. John didn't eat the last two days so the children could have more to eat. Now, without food or water, it would be difficult for any of them to survive. The sun beat down mercilessly during the day, and at night it was so cool it was difficult to sleep.

They rationed the gasoline. They would let the boat drift. Then when the sea became rough, they would use the engine to power the boat forward. When the food and water were gone, the gasoline also ran out. The travelers were drifting at the mercy of the sea.

The first day without food and water was difficult. The children had been brave, but they began to cry in the late afternoon. Thu held and rocked the youngest, the five-year-old. When the sun went down, it brought relief from the heat, but at night they had to contend with cold.

That evening a beautiful moon lit the sky. "I think that's the largest moon I've ever seen," John said to Mai. "It seems so near and so full, but when you're hungry, you could wish it was a big hunk of cheese."

"You're funny." Mai giggled.

"I know things are bad, Mai, but I believe God will somehow save us. I thought some ship would have already rescued us, but we haven't seen one, not even one. We've been praying." He turned imploring eyes toward her. "Why hasn't God answered our prayers?"

"I remember what Pastor Chanh said in one of his sermons. He said God answers prayers when He wants to not when we want Him to. He may be testing us."

"To be honest, I don't like it when God tests small children. With us, okay, but I resent it when it seems as if God is willing to let children die in order to test us."

"I know one thing for sure, John. God loves us, and He loves the children. I believe He'll do what's best for us. We can trust Him. Let's pray together."

For the next hour, John and Mai held hands and prayed together. Mai poured out her deepest feelings to the Lord, praying in Vietnamese, her heart language. As John prayed, lifting his voice skyward in the beautiful evening, he remembered a song they often sang in his home church in Hopewell, Texas. "Waft it on the rolling tide. Jesus saves! Jesus saves!"

John knew the words meant being saved from spiritual death, but he knew Jesus could—and did—also save people from physical death. Still, not everyone who called on the Lord was delivered from physical death, as was the case of Pastor Chanh.

"Mai, I believe if God still has something for us to do, you know, some mission for us to carry out, he won't let us die. Do you believe that?"

"Yes, I believe that as long as we are walking in His will, He will allow us to carry out His purpose for our lives."

"What about Pastor Chanh? He walked in God's will, but his life was cut short."

"John, many people have been touched by his sacrifice. Jesus was glorified in his death even as He was glorified by his life."

"Yeah, my life was certainly touched by Pastor Chanh's life and also by his death. I'll never forget him. Mai, I'm glad I can talk with you about spiritual things. I want to pray again. The Lord has formed a prayer in my heart from our talking together."

"Pray as the Lord leads you, John."

"Father, we ask you to save us, if it is Your will. You know best, and we give ourselves to know and do Your will, no matter what happens. Amen."

"Thanks, John. Let's try to get some sleep now."

John was awakened by bright sunlight. He went to sleep sitting against the side of the boat near the helm. The others were still sleeping. Mai cuddled near Thu and the children for warmth.

Peace of heart and mind filled John even though he knew the boat was moving at the mercy of the sea, and he didn't have the slightest idea where they were or where the sea would take them.

While John and his fellow boat crew faced uncertainty at sea, Captain Thong and his men faced a critical decision in their mission as guerrillas.

The battle-hardened North Vietnamese Rangers began closing in on the guerrillas. Captain Thong knew their time was limited. He sent word for all the guerrillas to meet a kilometer inland from the base camp.

The bloodied guerrillas gathered around him. "Men, the noose is getting tighter, and we can't stay here any longer without been killed or captured. The options, as I see them, are to join General Dao and his fighting Eighteenth Division at Xuan Loc, escape out by boat, or go back to our home village. Each of you can decide what you want to do."

Captain Thong opted to join General Dao at Xuan Loc. sixty three of the guerrillas volunteered to go with him. Lieutenant Dang had doubts about getting to Xuan Loc, so he decided to go to Phan Rang to try to escape by boat. Five men went with him. Three men returned to their villages.

Captain Thong and sixty of his men made it to Xuan Loc and joined General Dao and the fighting Eighteenth Division. They joined them in time to make one of the most valiant stands of the Vietnam War. Three were killed in skirmishes before they reached Xuan Loc.

Lieutenant Dang and his five men made it to Phan Rang where they managed to find a boat and launched out onto the South China Sea. After a harrowing week, they were picked up by a freighter that took them to America.

While Captain Thong and his men joined in on the battle at Xuan Loc, another battle raged on the seas, a battle to survive.

37

April 20, South China Sea

At the end of the third day without food and water, John knew that unless relief came within hours, the younger children would die. He could hear Hal's five-year-old son's weak plea, "*Nuoc, nuoc.*"

"He's pleading for water," Mai told John. "He will die unless we have water soon. John, I feel so helpless. All we can do is pray."

Hal's wife, Thu, fainted as she was trying to comfort the children. When she became conscious, she thrashed wildly and grabbed a bucket, attempting to get seawater. Knowing the danger of drinking the abundant yet salty water, Hal restrained her.

After the struggle, Thu laid totally still beside her youngest son. John wasn't sure if she was sleeping, unconscious, or dead. He checked to make sure. She was breathing normally. The heartrending situation left Hal so weak he could not sit up. He fell back on a makeshift pillow and managed a weak smile toward John and Mai.

Around ten o'clock in the evening, John felt the sea getting rougher. Waves pounded against the boat. Dark clouds shut out the light of the moon, and the wind became stronger. Suddenly a sheet of rain poured down on the boat.

"Up, everybody," John and Mai called to their sleeping boat-mates. "Let's get all the buckets and every container filled with rainwater. Hurry, hurry, hurry!"

They all summoned their last energy to capture the precious water in every available container. John stretched out a small tarp to catch the rain then drain it into the water can until it was more than half full.

The rain stopped as suddenly as it had started, and the sky cleared. Though it lasted only five minutes, the deluge had dumped lifesaving water into the boat. Everyone felt revived. Even the youngest had new life.

"Look," Hal shouted, "here's a fish in the boat!" Hal grabbed the flouncing foot-long fish and held it up in the light of the full moon for the others to see. He carefully cleaned the fish with his knife and cut it into edible bites. He asked John to say a prayer of blessing. John lifted his face toward heaven.

"Father, thank You for hearing and answering our calls for help. And thanks for the fish. Amen."

Hal distributed the pieces of fish. Everyone chewed slowly, savoring every bite. There was enough for each person to feel satisfied and refreshed. The children lay back down to sleep with new color in their faces.

The following day, with the sun high in the sky, Hal spotted a ship in the distance moving toward them. They yelled, waved, and made SOS signs. They could see men on the ship's deck looking toward them. But though the ship passed three hundred meters from their port side, the ship never slowed down.

The ship's refusal to help them had a demoralizing effect on the refugees. Hal's words matched his look of dejection. "Maybe no ship will stop for us."

Mai maintained her faith. "No, Hal, God will send a ship for us. We must not stop believing and asking God to deliver us. He will save us."

"Yes, Hal." John reaffirmed Mai's confidence. "The Lord is going to save us. He sent the water and the fish, didn't He? He will send a ship."

Hal was visibly encouraged. "You're right. The Lord did send us food and water. I believe He will send a ship."

The following two days the hot sun bore down on them relentlessly hour after hour. The extreme heat drove their thirst, and once again the water supply ran low. The children again felt hunger pangs.

On the morning of the third day after the rainstorm, Mai spotted a ship coming toward them. They all waved and yelled, but like the previous ship, it passed on without stopping. This time, though, no one spoke a negative word.

"I still believe the Lord will send a ship," Hal said.

Just a few seconds after Hal spoke, he stood up and exclaimed, "There's another ship coming from behind us! I believe this is God's ship for us!"

They all waved at the boat. Hal held up his five-year-old son, who joined in waving and calling for the ship to stop. It came within fifty meters of their boat and stopped. They could see the captain and ship's officers on the deck looking toward them and gesturing, apparently discussing what to do. Then the ship started its engines and moved on without attempting to help.

Stunned and devastated, the refugees fell to their knees crying out to the Lord. "Lord, please cause them to pity us. Lay us on their hearts, Lord. We're hungry and weary. And we're Your children. Please help us!" But despite the fervent prayers, the ship moved away. Drained physically and emotionally, everyone lay lifeless in the boat, the hot sun beating down on them.

Why was the ship of hope sailing away from them? They felt rejected as well as thirsty and hungry. Could they stay alive long enough to be rescued?

April 22, South China Sea

Lying in the helm end of the boat, John pushed himself up with exhausting effort. There was no movement from the others. He could feel the relentless heat of the afternoon sun. Heat waves danced in the air before him. His lips were cracked, and his tongue stuck to the roof of his mouth.

Something within cried out for him to take action. He had to survive. He had to make the others keep trying to live and not give up.

"Hal, Hal, get up. Hal, get up," he muttered with difficulty. He shook Hal's shoulder until Hal opened his eyes and looked up with a far away, dazed look. "Come on, Hal. Get up. Move your body. Sit up."

Hal slowly pushed himself to a sitting position.

"Hal, listen to me. We can't give up. We've come a long way, and we can't lie down and die in this boat. Somehow we're going to make it. Now help me get the others to sit up."

John knew if he could get everyone to move their bodies, even a little, it would help them mentally and physically. The younger children began to moan and cry out for water and food.

A plane flew overhead. It was so high they probably could not see the boat, but John stood up, waved, and yelled. His movement helped arouse the children and the other adults too. It even made him feel better. Three more planes flew overhead that afternoon, and each time John put on a theatrical performance of yelling and shouting at the pilots. "You can't leave us down here! Turn that thing around! At least drop us some food and water!"

Although John did it for the benefit of the others, especially the children, he felt pumped up after each performance. It made him feel more positive and hopeful. When the sun went down and the cool breeze brushed their faces, they felt revived and more hopeful.

"I almost gave up today," Hal admitted, "but I have hope. I believe the Lord will save us."

"Hal, I feel the same way," Mai agreed. "It was so disappointing to see the ship turn away. How could they just leave us to die? But like you, I believe the Lord will save us. He'll do it in His own time and His own way, but He will save us."

John added his affirmation. "Yeah, we thought for sure we were going to be picked up by that ship, but God has another ship for us. Let's keep trusting the Lord."

When darkness closed in on them, it brought a chilling coolness. Though the heat and emotion of the day had drained them, they bedded down for the night and slept peacefully.

John woke when the sun was well up over the horizon. He could feel it driving the cool out of the air. In another two hours, they would be bathed in another hot day.

Hal stirred and sat up. "John, I dreamed about food all night. I woke up with a hunger pain in the middle of my stomach."

"It had to be a dream. We don't have even a bite of food left. We need another fish to jump into the boat."

"John, what are we going to do? If we don't get help today, the children may die. They were very weak yesterday."

"Our only hope is in the Lord. There's no way we can save ourselves. We just have to depend on the Lord to save us."

"Thanks, John, for your faith and encouragement. Both you and Mai have been an inspiration to us. You just won't give up, and you encourage us not to give up but to keep on trusting."

"It's mutual, Hal. You are a good husband and father and a steady person. Without your help and knowledge, we would never have gotten this boat and escaped from Vietnam."

As the sun warmed the air, the children awoke. The younger ones cried for water and food. Thu rocked them in her arms to calm them. Mai tried to comfort the older ones. At midmorning, John heard the unmistakable sound of a helicopter. He saw it in the distance as it swirled toward them. He stood up and waved as vigorously as he could.

Evidently John caught the pilot's eye. He swerved off his course and came toward them. The helicopter hovered above them with deafening noise that caused the children to scream in fright. It slowly lowered until it was twenty-five feet over them. A rope ladder dropped out the door, and a soldier climbed down until he dropped into the boat.

He hollered to John over the noise. "Hey, you're an American, aren't you?"

"Yeah, I am. We left Vietnam almost two weeks ago, and we're out of food and water. Can you help us?"

"We'll try. We can take you in, but we can't take the others. We're on an aircraft carrier heading off the coast of South Vietnam to rescue Americans and Vietnamese escaping Saigon. Our commanding officer told us we can't pick up any boat people."

"Thanks for stopping," John said, devastated, "but I'll stay with my friends. These children will die if they don't get food and water today."

The soldier looked at the children. His face softened. "We can't let that happen. Tell you what. I'm going back up, and I'll lower all the food and water we have in the chopper, okay? Maybe that'll hold you till you get picked up or get where you're going. Good luck to you."

The soldier climbed back up the ladder. After a few minutes, he lowered a large basket of food and water. After John untied the basket, the soldier pulled the rope back into the helicopter, and it swirled away.

The basket held a two-gallon jug of water, boxes of C-rations, bread, packaged crackers and cheese, cans of beans, and GI candy bars. John enjoyed opening the packages of food for the children. They all ate, drank, and were refreshed.

"This is food from heaven." Hal grinned. "You know, I flew a helicopter for eight years, and I can really appreciate what that chopper crew did for us."

"These two gallons of water will not last long," John said. "We've already drunk almost a gallon. So let's try to drink as little as possible tomorrow. Maybe it'll last a few more days."

The precious water only lasted one more day. On the third day after the help from the helicopter the burning sun again left them thirsty and dry. They still had food, but when they ate it, it made them even thirstier.

"I thought the helicopter might have been the one to save us," Mai said. "But now I think the helicopter was sent to keep us alive until God's ship comes to pick us up."

Once again, the children began to cry, "*Nuoc, nuoc.*" John could see Hal's lips moving in prayer. Mai sat with her eyes closed, and John knew she was also praying. He closed his eyes and joined them in silent prayer. Hal's yell startled John out of his reverie.

"There's a ship! I believe this is God's ship!"

A large freighter moved slowly toward them. They all yelled and waved at the ship's crew. They could see them on the deck. The ship changed direction to avoid the boat and picked up speed. The waves from the ship tossed the small boat as it passed by them.

John, Hal, and Mai threw themselves on their knees. "Lord, have mercy on Your children. Touch the ship captain's heart. Send a ship to save us. Please, Lord."

John began to wonder if any ship would dare to take them in.

38

April 26, South China Sea

While they were on their knees crying out to the Lord, Hal's oldest daughter interrupted. "Dad, Dad, the ship has turned around and is coming back for us!"

They looked, and the ship was indeed coming back. Their pleas quickly turned into prayers of praise and thanksgiving. "Thank You, Lord Jesus! Thank You!"

The ship stopped fifty meters from them. A boat lowered from the ship with two seamen and two officers. They approached the refugees. One of the men recognized John was a westerner.

"Can you speak English?" he called.

"Yes, I'm an American."

"Where did your boat come from?"

"We came from Vietnam."

"What a mess over there. We're from Singapore, and we're heading back to our homeport. I assume you and the others would like to get on board with us."

"Yes, sir! We would very much like to go with you. We have barely survived since leaving Vietnam eighteen days ago."

"We'll take you to our ship. We can hoist you up to the deck two at a time in our passenger carriage. As for your boat, we'll need to sink it. Do you have any problem with that?"

"No, sir, not at all. It has fulfilled its mission."

"Well spoken, mate, well spoken."

On board the ship, John, Mai, Hal, and his family found the captain, ship's officers, and crew to be friendly and sympathetic. They were placed in rooms in the officers' quarters. They took hot showers, and crewmen brought them fresh clothes. They apologized for not having appropriate clothes for Mai and Thu, but the women were glad to put on men's clothes temporarily until their own could be washed. The clothes fit John and Hal perfectly.

Clean and dressed, they dove into trays of steaming food with tea and coffee. They ate, drank, and laughed together. It was like a good dream. John laughed and squeezed Mai's hand. "Pinch me, Mai. I may be dreaming. I can't believe this is real."

"No, John, you're not dreaming. You prayed that God would save us. It has happened. Wake up, and enjoy His blessings."

While Mai, Thu, and the children rested, John and Hal accepted the captain's invitation for coffee and sweets in his cabin. He was personable and inquisitive about what was happening in Vietnam. John and Hal shared some of their experiences and observations about the war. The captain was intrigued with John's story about coming back to find the girl he wanted to marry.

"I must say you have tenacity," he said. "And courage. Yes, courage. I think many a man would have bailed out against such odds and left his girlfriend behind."

The captain was pleased Hal could speak English well. He was impressed that Hal had flown helicopters for the South Vietnamese Army. "In your opinion," he asked Hal, "why are the South Vietnamese losing the war so quickly?" He listened intently as Hal shared his insights. He would have inside information to share with his peers in Singapore.

When the ship arrived in Singapore, the refugees were taken to old military barracks used to house immigration subjects waiting to be processed into the country. They had been renovated and were comfortable enough.

Since John had an American passport, he was taken to the American Embassy. He shared with the embassy officer about his escape from Vietnam with his girlfriend and his friend's family. The officer was sympathetic. "You know, if you can get a sponsor, we can get your Vietnamese friends to the States."

"What kind of sponsor do I need?"

"A church or some civic organization."

"That'll be no problem. My home church in Hopewell, Texas, will sponsor my friends. I'll call them tonight."

John didn't have time to think about his family. During his last days in Vietnam, he thought of little else besides struggling to survive. He didn't know how concerned they were because of not hearing from him.

39

Hopewell, Texas

Vance and Betty Gunter both worked tight schedules, but they watched TV and listened to radio news about Vietnam at every opportunity. They only heard from John twice since he first arrived in Saigon. Two weeks passed without any news from him.

Betty called her Sunday school class members to pray for John. She requested prayer at Wednesday evening prayer services. John was supposed to arrive in Dallas the first week in April, but there was no word from him. She went over her conversations with John in her mind. She felt sad because she did not support him in going back to Vietnam. She confided her regret to a close friend.

"Wanda, I'm so concerned about John. You know things are falling apart in Vietnam, and John is right in the middle of it. He was supposed to be back days ago, but we haven't heard a word from him."

"I'm listening to the news every chance I get," Wanda replied. "I'm also worried about John and what's happening over there. It looks as if South Vietnam is going to fall after all of our efforts to save it. That's a tragedy."

"Wanda, you know I really didn't support my son going back to get that Vietnamese girl. To be honest, I've cried about how I must have hurt John. He really loves the girl, and I should've been more supportive."

"Is the girl a Christian or some other religion?" Wanda asked.

"John said she's a strong Christian."

"You know that makes her our sister in Christ, doesn't it?"

"Yeah, you're right. I'd never thought of her in that way. John said there are a lot of Christians in Vietnam."

"I just heard on the news thousands are fleeing South Vietnam by boat," Wanda said. "Most of them are trying to get to America. Pastor Roger said the association is already planning on sponsoring some Vietnamese families."

"Did Pastor Roger say our church is going to sponsor a family?"

"I heard it probably will come up for a vote in the coming business meeting. I've also heard that a number of our church members are against us sponsoring Vietnamese."

"What do you think about it?"

"As the Women's Missionary Union president, I'd resign if I couldn't vote for sponsoring a Vietnamese family."

"Why do you say that?"

"If I believe in carrying the gospel to people all over the world then refuse to take in people God brings to us, I'm not practicing what I claim to believe."

"I see what you mean. What if John shows up with a Vietnamese family? Wouldn't it be awful if we refused to sponsor them?"

"Yes, it would be sad, and it'd be inexcusable to refuse people who need our help at this critical time of their lives."

"Wanda, you're right. I'm glad you're my friend and that you see things from God's point of view and not man's. I appreciate your convictions."

"My convictions are based on the Bible. That's why I believe we should have a missionary heart. You know we have more than thirty missionaries in Vietnam, don't you?"

"I didn't know that. What's happened to them?"

"Most of them, as I understand, have been evacuated."

"Something else just occurred to me. We send missionaries to Vietnam to share the gospel of Christ's love with the Vietnamese people, and then what if we reject these same people that are sent here to us? Wouldn't that be terrible?"

"Betty, would you be willing to share with our WMU group a few minutes this coming Monday evening? Just share what you just told me."

"I'll be glad to."

The First Church of Hopewell held a special business meeting Sunday night. Word had spread around that the sponsoring of a Vietnamese family was on the agenda. At least three of the deacons were against sponsoring, as one deacon put it, "any foreign family." A good number of people in the congregation were neutral or indifferent. The Women's Missionary Union believed the church had a mission opportunity and should take the lead in sponsoring a family.

Their pastor, Brother Roger, had led in urging churches to sponsor refugees. It would be an embarrassment for him if his own church refused. Before the business meeting, his conversation with the Chairman of the Deacons told him he faced that possibility.

The Chairman had stated his reasons for opposing the sponsorship of a Vietnamese family. "They're not like us," he stated. "They speak and think differently. And most have a different religion. They're Buddhist, Hindu, or something. They're all mixed up."

Pastor Roger said, "Brother, that's why we send missionaries over to Vietnam, so they might hear the truth of the gospel and believe in Christ. Now God is bringing them to us here in America."

"But some of 'em may be Communists. You can't tell what their motives are in coming over here. Our soldiers who went to Vietnam say you can't tell a Viet Cong from anyone else. We don't need to take 'em in. Let 'em stay over there."

"Brother, most of the refugees coming here have lost everything they owned, even members of their families. Some will be imprisoned or killed if they stay because they worked closely with us. Now is the best time to share our love and the love of Jesus with them."

"Well, Pastor, I just can't see us taking in a foreign family now. We have so many needy families all around us in this town. Families from here. We know them. And they need our help from time to time. It doesn't make sense to me for us to take in a bunch of foreigners."

Pastor Roger called the Sunday night business meeting into session. He introduced, the Associational Director of Missions, to give an overview of the proposed program to sponsor Vietnamese refugees.

He summarized the association's proposal to meet the needs of hundreds of refugees pouring into the States temporarily housed in Camp Chaffee, Arkansas, and Camp Pendleton, California. He closed his presentation with this appeal:

"Brothers and Sisters of First Church of Hopewell, I encourage you to take the lead in this needy and timely program of meeting the desperate needs of hundreds of refugees coming our way. Your participation will encourage others to join in this great ministry."

One of the deacons made the motion that the church sponsor a Vietnamese family, or families, as the church was able. It was seconded by Vance Gunter. Every member was given the opportunity to speak for or against it. It proved to be a hot issue.

The Chairman of Deacons spoke against the motion. He was influential in the church, and his talk drew many amens. Betty Gunter stood. "I'm in favor of this motion. If we say we are a mission minded church, yet we turn away these refugees, then we're not practicing what we preach."

The meeting went well past the usual closing time as member after member got up and voiced their convictions. Some people spoke who had never said a word in a business meeting before. It seemed to Pastor Roger it was going to be a hung jury, for the sides were pretty even. He feared the motion would not pass. He began to sense the issue might cause serious division in the church. He considered how he could get someone to table the motion.

Suddenly the swinging doors of the sanctuary opened, and Debra Gunter rushed in. Every eye was upon her as she looked for her parents. She motioned for them to come to the back of the church. Absolute silence gripped the congregation as Debra whispered to her parents, Vance and Betty.

They heard Betty let out a cry. Was it joy or grief? Tears coursed down her face. Vance and Betty returned to their seats. Brother Roger cleared his throat.

"Brother Vance and Sister Betty, would you like to share something with us?"

"John is safe in Singapore," Betty blurted between sobs. "He came out in a boat with some Vietnamese."

The church stood as one and applauded.

Vance Gunter made his way to the front and requested permission to address the congregation. He struggled with tears as he tried to speak. "John asked Debra … to ask us as a church … if we would sponsor his sweetheart and the family that came out with him in the boat."

The church sat stunned. You could have heard a pin drop. Brother Roger rose and stood beside Vance Gunter, tears flowing down his face along with many in the congregation.

"All in favor of the motion say amen," the pastor said.

People all over the neighborhood could have heard the resounding roar of assent. There were no opposing votes.

40

Singapore

"There's an American missionary here from Vietnam helping with Vietnamese refugees," the embassy official told John. "He comes by every day. He can also help you."

John was immediately interested. "What is his name?"

"Um, let's see. What is his name? Oh yeah. Burt is his name. Jeff Burt and his wife Ann."

"I know them!" John exclaimed. "I've been in their home. I want to see them."

When John finished filling out papers and started to leave, Jeff Burt walked in the door. Apparently he did not immediately recognize John since he was not expecting to see him in Singapore. However, alerted to the fact that Jeff was in the area, John recognized him at once.

"Jeff Burt! Am I glad to see you! I'm glad you and your family made it out of Nha Trang. I was worried about you."

After shaking hands with John, the light of recognition broke over Jeff's face. "John! What a surprise seeing you here! Did your Vietnamese sweetheart come with you?

"Yes, she did, and she's over in the immigration barracks with a family that came out with us."

"Wait till I tell Ann. She'll be so excited to know you're here. We've gotta get together and share our experiences. We can't wait to meet Mai."

Early that evening, Jeff and Ann met John, Mai, and Hal's family in the immigration cafeteria. They shared experiences for several hours. They laughed, cried, and rejoiced together over the tumultuous experiences of the last forty days. Jeff and Ann promised to visit them in Texas.

Jeff encouraged John and Hal. "Although I've been here just a short while, I've become acquainted with some of the embassy people. I'll try to get them to expedite your going on to the States."

The next day when John called his family, Debra, his sister, was the only one at home. She told him their mom and dad had gone to work.

"Deb, did the church vote to sponsor Mai and Hal's family? They did? That's great! Would you ask the church to send a telegram to the American Embassy in Singapore to confirm? Thanks, Deb. Tell Mom and Dad hi for me. See you soon."

Early the following morning, John waited at the gate of the American Embassy until it opened. Mrs. Pringle, the officer in charge of refugees, saw him.

"I believe you're John Gunter. I'm Judy Pringle, and I'm assigned to help with refugees. We just received a telegram from your church confirming that they will sponsor your Vietnamese friends."

"Thanks, Mrs. Pringle. That's good news."

"You can go to the barracks and bring your friends here. I'll give you a letter to show to the Singapore immigration officials."

By three o'clock that afternoon, the process was completed. The next morning they boarded a Pan Am flight to Honolulu. Jeff and Ann Burt saw them off at the airport.

At Honolulu, they took an American Airlines flight to Dallas. John's mom, dad, pastor, and friends met them in Dallas and took them to Hopewell. The church and town turned out to welcome them. The pastor had called ahead to have the people assemble at the church for a grand potluck dinner extravaganza. TV stations from Dallas, Ft. Worth, and Mineral Wells were there to record the event. The town mayor and other local politicians were all present.

John was amazed at the reception. He thought it ironic that when he came back from Vietnam in 1973 no one welcomed him except his immediate family. As a matter of fact, two college students accosted him in the airport at Dallas and conveyed their dislike to him about America's role in Vietnam.

Although John was gone less than two months, it seemed like years. He had set his goal to be in Vietnam forty days, but so many events were packed into that short time it was like an eternity.

He smiled at Mai standing beside him as they met new friends and greeted old ones. He went to Vietnam to bring her back, and by God's grace and goodness, he accomplished his mission.

EPILOGUE

Vietnam

Captain Thong and his men joined with the courageous Eighteenth Division, led by the colorful General Le Minh Dao, to fight in the largest and fiercest battle of the Indo-China War.

The South Vietnamese forces who retreated to Bien Hoa surrendered to the North Vietnamese.

The Eighteenth Division fought gallantly and expended most of their ammunition and strength in the battle. They gave their all in a valiant last stand to defend the capital, Saigon.

General Le Minh Dao knew his troops were exhausted. For him to call upon them to continue to resist would mean death for most of them. Thus he met with North Vietnam's General Dung to work out terms for surrender. The terms were simple. If they laid down their arms, they could go home to their families.

General Dao agreed to the terms. However, they were not kept by the North Vietnamese. General Dao and other high-ranking officers in his division were later sent to prison. The majority of the troops were sent to reeducation camps. As a soldier, General Dung himself admired and respected the gallant stand made by the enemy. He would have stood by the surrender terms. But once the political arm took over, he did not have a say in what happened to the prisoners.

Captain Thong was sent to the Hanoi Hilton where he underwent tortuous treatment for fifteen plus years before his release. Brenda, his wife, continually fought for his release. Every time she heard of an US Delegation going to Hanoi, she implored them to put in a word for Captain Thong's release. Her pleas kept Captain Thong alive.

Finally, in the early nineties Captain Thong was released from prison. Today, he lives in Houston, Texas with his wife Brenda. Although he has poor health, he stays busy at his job working on computers.

Texas

Just as John expected, the Gunter family members were enthralled with Mai. Debra and Mai quickly became friends. Debra took Mai about town to the drive-ins and cafes where her friends hung out and proudly introduced her to them. Mai became somewhat of a celebrity in Hopewell. Her arrival in the States after such harrowing experiences at sea captured the attention of the media and the imagination of the people.

Betty Gunter enjoyed introducing Mai to all the gadgets and appliances in the kitchen and house. She showed her how to cook John's favorite foods such as lasagna, potato salad, and fried chicken. Betty took Mai to the Woman's Missionary Union meeting at church and was pleased that Mai was willing to share with the group about her church and family in Vietnam.

Hal, Thu, and their four children moved into a house owned by the church. The house formerly served as a parsonage, and it made a wonderful guest house. The women in the church and community filled the pantry with cans and boxes of food, including a fifty-pound sack of Thai rice.

The women organized a time to teach Thu English. Teenagers taught the children. Hal's two daughters, thirteen-year-old Tri and ten-year-old Hanh, were ready and eager to learn their new language. They already knew some words they learned from their father.

John and Mai planned their wedding for the first Sunday in June. John asked Hal to be his best man, and Mai wanted Thu to be her matron of honor. They were pleased to be asked to help join John and Mai together.

Betty Gunter and her lady friends from church reveled at the opportunity to prepare the wedding. With Mai, Thu, and her daughters, they loaded into two vans and went to Dallas to help choose the wedding dress and other trappings. The trip took all day, but the ladies returned excited about the dresses and their part in choosing them. They told their families that Mai looked like a beautiful doll in her wedding dress.

The shopping trip and other wedding preparations were reported in the "About Town" column of the twice-weekly local paper, the *Hopewell Times*. The wedding became the chief topic of conversation in Hopewell.

The event took on a celebrity status, adding to the excitement for the local population. The Ft. Worth Star Telegram and the Dallas Morning News, as well as TV stations in several cities, would cover the wedding.

On the big day, the crowd packed the auditorium and spilled into the churchyard. Television and newspaper reporters pushed into the building to set up their equipment. White lilies and red roses adorned the sanctuary with white and red candles in elegant candelabras. John's pastor took his place on the platform followed by John and Hal. Then all eyes turned to the back of the church in anticipation of the bride's entrance.

The crowd stood up as the organ struck the first notes of "Here Comes the Bride." A buzz swept through the auditorium when Mai, accompanied by Vance Gunter, came down the aisle. Vance told her he would be honored to escort her since her father could not be present. He walked proudly beside the beautiful bride.

Like most weddings, the ceremony was over in minutes. The reception in the fellowship hall lasted more than an hour. After the tossing of the bridal bouquet, the bride and groom made their departure amid the traditional shower of rice.

John returned to his previous job and helped Hal also get a job there. After five years, John and Hal decided to start their own trucking company. They named their firm Trusted Tiger. By the early nineties, one could see their trailers painted with racing tigers on interstates and state highways throughout America.

John and Mai had two boys and a girl. Hal's two daughters graduated from college and went to work with large companies as computer specialists. His two sons studied engineering at Texas A&M.

In 1995, John, Mai, and their children, along with Hal, Thu, and their children, returned to visit Vietnam. Still in good health, Mai's parents continued to do some work on the farm. Her siblings were all married. The two daughters lived with their families in Dalat, and the two sons lived in Saigon and worked with a thriving export company.

Both Hal and Thu's parents died in the early nineties.

Dao still managed her inn. Hien, married with three children, owned and managed a large travel agency in Dalat. He still lived in Lien in order to be near his beloved mother. He spoke English well and was proud to be able to spend time conversing with John.

"John, you were one of my best teachers and friends," he said. "My oldest son is named after you."

John and Mai enjoyed staying on the farm with the Tuans. One evening as the sun was setting, John and Mai walked hand in hand to their former picnic spot. John remembered the times he worked in the fields with Mai and her family. He recalled all his narrow escapes from death and how God overshadowed him during those forty days in Vietnam that seemed like an eternity.